DAYBREAK

AMS PRESS
NEW YORK

ARTHUR SCHNITZLER
DAYBREAK

Translated from the German by
WILLIAM A. DRAKE

SIMON AND SCHUSTER

Copyright © 1927, 1954 by William A. Drake

Reprinted from the edition of 1927: New York

First AMS edition published in 1971

Manufactured in the United States of America

International Standard Book Number: 0-404-05615-6

Library of Congress Catalog Card Number: 73-175443

PT
2638
N5
D2x

AMS PRESS INC.
NEW YORK, N.Y. 10003

DAYBREAK

I

"Lieutenant! . . . Lieutenant! . . . Lieutenant!"

Only after the third call did the young officer move, stretch himself, and turn his head toward the door. Still drunk with sleep, he muttered among the pillows: "What's up?" Then, having roused himself, and seeing that it was only his orderly standing in the shadows near the half-opened door, he shouted:

"What the devil do you want, so early in the morning?"

"There is a gentleman below in the court, Sir, who wishes to speak with the Lieutenant."

"What kind of a gentleman? What time

is it, then? Haven't I told you often enough that I don't wish to be disturbed on Sundays?"

The orderly stepped over to the bed and handed Wilhelm a visiting card.

"Do you take me for an owl, you blockhead? Do you think I can read in the dark? Put up the shades!"

Even before the command was finished, Joseph had opened the inner shutters of the window and drawn up the dirty white curtain. The Lieutenant, half sitting in the bed, was now able to read the name on the card. He let it fall on the covers, looked at it again, ran his fingers through the morning dishevel of his blond, close-cropped hair, and considered hastily:

"Send him away?—Impossible!—There's no occasion for that. If I receive a person, that certainly does not imply that I am intimate with him. Anyway, it was only because of debts that he had to quit. Others simply have better luck. But what can he want of me?"

He turned again to the orderly:

"How does he look, the Lieut— I mean, Herr von Bogner?"

The orderly replied with a broad, but somewhat melancholy smile:

"If I may be permitted to say so, Sir, the Lieutenant looked better in his uniform."

Wilhelm was silent for a moment. Then he sat up more comfortably in the bed:

"Well, ask him to come in. And beg the Lieutenant to be so good as to excuse me if I am not yet quite dressed. And see here—this applies to every one!—if any of the other gentlemen should ask for me—Lieutenant Hoechster, or Lieutenant Wengler, or the Captain, or anybody at all—I am not at home. Do you understand?"

As Joseph closed the door behind him, Wilhelm quickly pulled on his blouse, arranged his hair and, crossing to the window, looked down into the still deserted courtyard of the barracks; and as he saw his former comrade below, walking up and down with bowed head, his stiff black hat pressed down on his forehead, in an unbuttoned yellow overcoat, with brown and somewhat dusty oxfords, he grew sick at heart. He opened the window and was almost on the point of beckoning to him and greeting him aloud; but at that moment his orderly approached the waiting man, and Wilhelm observed, on the painfully drawn face of his old friend, the emotion with which he awaited the answer. Since it was favourable, Bogner's features lightened in a smile, and he disappeared with the orderly through the door beneath Wilhelm's window—which the latter now closed, as though surmising that the coming conversation would doubtless make such a precaution necessary. And suddenly the odour of the forest and of spring was gone—an odour which permeated the barracks courtyard on such Sunday mornings as this, but, curiously enough, could hardly ever be noticed on the week-days. Let happen what may, thought Wilhelm—and what could happen, anyway?—I'm going to Baden today, and I'll have luncheon at the Stadt Wien—that is, if they don't keep me to dine at the Kessners', as they did the last time.

"Come in!" And with a rather exaggerated cordiality, Wilhelm held out his hand. "How are you, Bogner? I'm delighted to see you. Won't you take off your coat? Yes, look round; everything the same as ever. The place hasn't gotten any larger. 'But there's room in the smallest hut for a happy . . .'"

Otto smiled politely, as if he were aware of Wilhelm's embarrassment and wished to help him out of it.

"I hope," he said, "that your quotation about the 'smallest hut' usually fits better than it does at the present moment."

Wilhelm laughed, more loudly than was necessary.

"Unfortunately, not often. I live quite simply. I assure you that, for six weeks at least, there has not been a woman in this room. Plato was a rascal, compared with me. But won't you sit down?" He took some linen from a chair and threw it onto the bed. "And mayn't I offer you a cup of coffee?"

"Thank you, Kasda, don't trouble yourself. I have already had breakfast. . . . A cigarette, though, if you don't mind . . ."

Wilhelm would not permit Otto to use his own case, but pointed to the smoking stand, where lay an open box of cigarettes. Wilhelm offered his guest a light. Otto inhaled a few draughts, when his glance chanced to fall upon a well-known picture which hung on the wall above the black leather divan—an old-time representation of an officers' steeplechase.

"Well, now, tell me of yourself," said Wilhelm. "How have you been? Why has no one heard from you in such a long time? When we parted, two or three years ago, you did promise that, now and then—"

But Otto interrupted him:

"It was better, perhaps, that I did not

let anybody see or hear of me. And it certainly would have been better if I had not been obliged to come here today." And—rather surprisingly, Wilhelm thought—he sat down in a corner of the divan, the opposite corner of which was filled with a clutter of books. "For, as you may well imagine, Willi"—he spoke rapidly and sharply—"my visit today, at this unusual hour—I know you like to sleep late on Sundays—my visit has, of course, a purpose. Otherwise, I should not have permitted myself—to be brief, I have come in the name of our old friendship, since unluckily I can no longer say, 'our comradeship.' You needn't grow so pale, Willi. It's not so dangerous. It's a question of a few gulden, which I simply must have by tomorrow morning. Otherwise, there is nothing left for me but to do that"—his voice rose in a military harshness—"that which I should have done two years ago, had I been wise."

"What utter nonsense!" Wilhelm observed, in a tone of annoyance, tempered by friendly embarrassment.

The orderly brought in breakfast and disappeared. Willi poured the coffee. He was sensible of an acrid taste in his mouth, and it vexed him that he had not been able to complete his morning toilet. However, he had planned to take a Turkish bath on his way to the station. If he reached Baden by noon, there would still be time. He had made no definite appointment; and if he were to arrive late, even if he were not to come at all, nobody would think it strange —neither the gentlemen at the Café Schopf, nor Fräulein Kessner; though perhaps her mother, who was not at all a bad sort, would wonder why he had not come.

"Please, please go on," he said to Otto, who had not yet put the cup to his lips.

The latter took a hasty sip, and began at once:

"I shall tell it briefly. Perhaps you know that, for the last three months, I have held the position of cashier in the office of an electrical installation company. But how should you know that? You do not even know that I am married—that I have a four year old boy. You see, I had him already when I was still here. Not a soul knew of it. Well, I did not have such a fortunate time of it. I fancy you will understand. And particularly this last winter. The boy was ill. The details can't be of any interest to you—but then, on several occasions, I was forced to borrow a little out of the drawer. I always put it back at the proper time. But this time, as my luck would have it, the circumstances were quite exceptional, and . . ."—he paused for a moment, while Wilhelm stirred his coffee with his spoon—"and, to make matters worse, by mere chance I have learned that a thorough inspection is to be made, beginning with the factory. The auditor will come Monday, that is, tomorrow. We are a branch, you understand, and we take care of only very small accounts. As a matter of fact, it is only a mere nothing that I owe—nine hundred and sixty gulden. I might say, a thousand—that is about the same. But nine hundred and sixty is the amount. And I must have them by tomorrow morning, at half-past-nine. Otherwise . . . Well, in any case, you would be doing me a really tremendous favour, Willi, if you could spare me this sum."

Suddenly he could go no further. Willi was a little abashed for him, not so much on account of the petty infidelity or fraud —for it was really fraudulence!—of which his former comrade had been guilty, but rather because the sometime Lieutenant Otto von Bogner, who, only two years ago, had still been a smart, popular and well-situated officer, now sat, pale and crumpled, leaning against the end of the divan, unable to continue on account of his tears.

He placed his hand on Otto's shoulder. "See here, Otto," he said, "you must not abandon hope so quickly!"

And, as Otto, with a desolate, frightened air, looked up at this somewhat inauspicious beginning, he added: "That is, I am myself somewhat low in funds just now. My whole fortune consists of about one hundred gulden. One hundred and twenty, to be as accurate as you have been. It goes without saying that the entire amount is at your disposal, down to the last copper. It isn't enough, of course. But if we set ourselves to it, we shall certainly be able to think of some way out."

Again, Otto cut him short:

"You may be sure that I have just about exhausted all the possible ways. We must not waste time racking our brains unnecessarily—especially, since I already have a definite suggestion."

Wilhelm looked at him intently.

"Try to imagine, Willi, that you yourself were in just such a difficulty. What would you do?"

"I don't quite understand," Wilhelm replied, a little stiffly.

"Naturally, I know perfectly well that you have never taken money from a stranger's cash drawer—that is something that can only happen to a man in civil life. Agreed! Still, for the sake of argument, if, for some less criminal reason, it became absolutely necessary for you to obtain a certain sum of money, to whom would you go?"

"I beg your pardon, Otto, but I have never thought of such a necessity arising, and I hope . . . Of course, I have sometimes had debts. I do not deny that. Only last month Hoechster had to help me out with fifty gulden, which, of course, I paid him back on the first. That is how I chance to be so short just now. But a thousand gulden—a thousand!—I certainly do not know where I could lay hold of such an amount."

"You really do not?" said Otto, looking him squarely in the eye.

"That is what I said."

"And your uncle?"

"What uncle?"

"Your Uncle Robert."

"What makes you think of him?"

"Why, it is perfectly natural. He has helped you out on several occasions. And you have a regular allowance from him, as well."

"There has been no allowance for a long time," Willi replied, annoyed by the hardly appropriate tone of his former comrade. "And not only has there been no allowance. Uncle Robert has turned out an eccentric. In point of fact, I haven't set eyes on him in a year. And the last time I asked him for a little something—as a very special accommodation—well, he practically threw me out of the house."

"Indeed, is that so?" Bogner passed his hand across his forehead. "So you would consider that possibility absolutely ruled out?"

"I hope you don't doubt my word!" Wilhelm replied, somewhat sharply.

Suddenly Bogner forsook the corner of the divan, pushed the table aside, and went over to the window.

"We must take a chance," he declared,

with assurance. "Yes, pardon me, but we must! The worst that could happen would be that he may refuse, and it is possible that he may not be too polite about it. I grant you that. But, as compared with what will probably happen to me if I do not succeed in gathering together a few paltry gulden by tomorrow morning, that is only a minor annoyance."

"Very likely!" said Wilhelm, "but an annoyance absolutely to no good purpose. If there were only the slightest chance— well, I certainly trust that you have no doubt of my good intentions. The devil take it! There must be other possibilities! For example—you mustn't be angry; I just chanced to think of him!—how about your cousin Guido, who has the estate near Amstetten?"

"I assure you, Willi," Bogner replied, calmly, "that there is no possibility of getting anything from him. If there were, I should not be here. In other words, there is not a person on the face of the earth——"

Willi suddenly lifted his finger, as if an idea had come to him.

Bogner gazed at him, in eager expectation.

"If you were to try Rudy Hoechster! Only a few months ago, as it happens, he received an inheritance! Twenty or twenty-five thousand gulden! Something must be left of all that!"

Bogner's face clouded, and he answered, with some hesitation:

"I have already written to Hoechster. Three weeks ago, when the situation was not yet so serious. And I asked him for much less than a thousand. He didn't even answer me. So, you see, your uncle affords really the only way out." And, as Willi shrugged his shoulders, he added: "I know him, Willi—a very sympathetic, charming old gentleman. We were at the theatre together several times, and at Riedhof's—he no doubt will remember! Good God, you certainly cannot tell me that he has suddenly become another man!"

Willi interrupted him, impatiently:

"And still it seems that he has! I myself don't know what has really happened to him. But it's not uncommon for people in their fifties and sixties to change very conspicuously. I can say no more than this— that for fifteen months or more, I have not entered his house, and that, moreover, I shall never enter it again, under any circumstances."

Bogner stared fixedly ahead of him. Presently he raised his head, gazing beyond Willi as if the latter did not exist, and said:

"Well, I am sorry to have troubled you. Good-bye!"

And, taking his hat, he turned to the door.

"Otto!" Willi cried, "I have had another idea!"

"Another! What does it matter!"

"But you must listen to me, Bogner! I

Daybreak

am going to the country today—to Baden. There, on Sunday afternoons, in the Café Schopf, we sometimes gamble a little—a friendly break at Vingt-et-un or else Baccarat, one or the other. Of course, I take only a very small part in the game, or perhaps I even stay out of it altogether. I have played three or four times, and then only for the fun of it. The banker is Tugut, the Army Doctor; Lieutenant Wimmer is usually there also, and Greising, of the 77th. . . . You don't know him. He is detailed in Baden on some outside work—on account of an old scandal. And then, there are a few civilians—a local lawyer, the manager of the theatre, an actor, and an old man, a certain Consul Schnabel. He is having an affair with a musical comedy singer—a chorus girl, in fact. These are the regulars. Two weeks ago, Tugut raked in three thousand gulden at a single sitting. We played on the open verandah until six o'clock in the morning—the birds gave us a musical accompaniment to our play. I have only my endurance to thank for the hundred and twenty that I now have—otherwise, I should be quite penniless. Now, do you know what I am going to do, Otto? One hundred of this hundred and twenty gulden, I shall risk for you. The chance is not overwhelmingly favourable, I know, but only a few days ago, Tugut sat down with fifty and got up with three thousand. And there is still another point: in the last few months, I have had no luck at all in love. Perhaps we can place more reliance upon a proverb than we can in people."

Bogner said nothing.

"Well!" Willi demanded. "What do you think of my idea?"

Bogner shrugged his shoulders.

"Whatever may come of it, I thank you. I thank you very much. Of course, I do not refuse. Still——"

"Naturally, I can't make any guarantees," Willi broke in, with a brave flourish of vivacity. "Still, I'm not risking very much. And if I win, if it's only one thousand—at least one thousand of it belongs to you. And if I should happen to make an extraordinary killing——"

"Don't promise too much," Otto remarked, with a melancholy smile. "But I mustn't detain you any longer. And for my own sake, too! Tomorrow morning, I shall take the liberty—rather . . . I shall be waiting, tomorrow morning, at half-past-eight, over there, near the Alser Church." As Willi attempted to reply, Bogner silenced him with a gesture, and added quickly: "Besides, I do not propose to be idle, upon my own account. I still possess a fortune of seventy gulden. I shall risk them this afternoon, at the races."

He crossed over to the window with quick steps, and looked down into the courtyard of the barracks.

"The air is very clear!" he said, and his mouth was twisted in a smile of bitter sarcasm as he spoke. Then, having given Willi his hand, he departed.

Wilhelm sighed softly, pondered for a

moment, and then began to prepare himself to go out. He was not very well satisfied with the condition of his uniform. Should he win today, he was determined to buy himself at least a new cape. Because of the lateness of the hour, he abandoned the idea of a Turkish bath. But in any case, he would take a fiacre to the train. Two gulden, more or less, did not really matter today.

II

When, at noon, Wilhelm left the train at Baden, he was in excellent spirits. At the station in Vienna, he had had an extremely cordial conversation with Lieutenant-Colonel Wositzky, who, when on duty, was the most disagreeable of men; and in his coupé there had been two young girls, who had carried on such an animated flirtation with him that he was relieved when they did not get out at his station, since otherwise he would not have been able to carry out the program which he had determined upon for this day. Despite his amiable mood, he was still inclined to hold some reproach against his former comrade, Bogner, not so much because he had taken the money from the drawer—an occurrence which, since it was due to his unfortunate circumstances, was to a certain extent excusable—but more particularly because of the stupid gambling scandal by which he had, three years before, cut short his promising career. An officer, certainly, ought to know just how far he can let himself go. For example, three weeks ago, when ill-luck dogged him, he had simply gotten up from the card table, in spite of the fact that Consul Schnabel, in a most charming manner, had offered him his purse. In fact, he had always known how to resist temptations, and he had always contrived to make ends meet on his small salary and the petty allowances which he had received, first from his father, and, after the latter's death as a Lieutenant-Colonel at Temesvar, from his Uncle Robert. And when these additional remittances had ceased to come, he had known how to conform to his slighter means—he had diminished the frequency of his visits to the coffee house, cut down his purchases, saved on cigarettes, and determined that women, in the future, must not cost him anything. Only three months ago, a little adventure, which had begun most auspiciously, had ended in disaster, for the sole reason that Willi had been absolutely unable to pay for a dinner for two people.

He became truly sad, as he mused. He had never been quite so conscious of the narrowness of his circumstances as he was today—this beautiful, spring day!—as he wandered through the fragrant gardens of the country estate in which the Kessner family lived and which they doubtless owned, and considered that his cape was a little shabby, that his trousers were beginning to shine somewhat at the knees, and that his cap was too low, much lower than the newest officers' style. And today he realised, too, for the first time, that he was ashamed of the fact that he hoped for an invitation to remain to dinner; or rather, he was ashamed of the fact that this expectation should have presented itself to him with the urgency of hope.

Nevertheless, he was by no means displeased when his hope was fulfilled, not only because the meal was delightfully appointed and the wine excellent, but likewise because of Fräulein Emily, who sat at his right, and who made an exceedingly agreeable neighbour at table, with her friendly glances and her familiar touches, which might, however, always be considered as merely accidental. He was not the only guest. There was also a young attorney, whom Herr Kessner had brought from Vienna, and who understood how to lead the conversation into light, gay, and somewhat ironical channels. Toward Willi, Herr Kessner was polite, but somewhat cold; he was not greatly pleased, on the whole, at these Sunday visits of the Lieutenant, who had taken entirely too literally the casual invitation to stop in some time for tea, which the ladies of the house had extended to him when he had been presented at a ball during the last Carnival. Even the still pretty Frau Kessner apparently retained no recollection of the fact that, two weeks ago, seated on a secluded bench in the garden, she had neglected to withdraw herself from the Lieutenant's bold embrace until the sound of approaching footsteps on the gravel path had been heard. The first subject of conversation at the table had to do with a suit, concerning some matter which the lawyer had been administering in behalf of Herr Kessner's factory; and the Lieutenant was annoyed because he had not been able to understand all of the legal expressions. Then the talk drifted to country life and summer travel, and in this Willi was able to take part. Two years ago, he had participated in the Imperial manœuvres in the Dolomites, and he now told of camping out in the open, of the two dark-haired daughters of an innkeeper at Kastelruth, who had been called the Two Medusæ, on account of their unapproachability, and of a certain Field-Marshal, who had, as it were, before Willi's own eyes, fallen into disgrace in consequence of a bungled cavalry attack. And, as ever after his third or fourth glass of wine, he grew more and more unaffected, sprightly, even witty. He could note how he gradually conquered Herr Kessner, how the lawyer's tone gradually became less ironical, how Frau Kessner's face began to glow with a certain memory, and how the thrilling touch of Emily's knee no longer was at pains to dissemble its intimacy as the grace of chance.

Punctually with the black coffee, an elderly, rather corpulent lady appeared, accompanied by her two daughters. Willi was presented to the newcomers as "our dancer at the Industries Ball." It soon developed that the three ladies had also resided in South Styria two years ago; and was it not the Lieutenant whom they had seen galloping past their hotel in Seis one beautiful summer day, on a coal-black horse? This Willi was reluctant to deny, although none knew better than he how unlikely it was that an obscure Lieutenant of the 89th Infantry might have been seen galloping on a proud charger through any village, in Styria or elsewhere.

The two young ladies were attractively clad in white. Fräulein Kessner, in a light, rose-coloured frock, was between them: and thus all three ran mischievously over the lawn.

"Somewhat like the Three Graces, aren't they?" the lawyer observed. His tone was again ironic, and the Lieutenant was strongly tempted to demand: "What do you mean by that?" But it was easy to pass over the remark, for Fräulein Emily, out on the lawn, had turned round and was beckoning him to join her. She was blond, slightly taller than he, and it was presumable that she might expect quite a considerable dowry. But it was still a long way to that; even to the imagining of such agreeable possibilities: and meanwhile, the thousand gulden required by his unfortunate comrade had to be procured before tomorrow morning.

So there was nothing left for him to do,

in the interests of the former Lieutenant von Bogner, but to make his excuses at the very moment when the entertainment was becoming most diverting. He was made to believe that they would sincerely have liked him to remain, and he assured them of his own regret; but, unfortunately, he had made an appointment, and he felt compelled, moreover, to visit a comrade who was taking a cure in the Military Hospital for an old case of rheumatism. Again, the lawyer laughed ironically. With a smile full of promise, Frau Kessner asked if the visit must take up the whole afternoon. Willi shrugged his shoulders uncertainly. At any rate, everybody would be happy to see him again this evening, in the event he should manage to get free.

As he left the house, two elegant young men rode up in a fiacre. This did not please Willi at all. What might not happen in this house, while he was forced to sit in a wretched coffee house, earning a thousand gulden for the sake of a broken comrade!

Daybreak

Would it not be much more wise to abandon the whole affair, and to return in half an hour, after his pretended visit to his sick friend, to the Three Graces in the beautiful garden? All the more wise, he reflected, with some complacency, since, by the law of the adage, his chances of winning at cards must assuredly have been considerably reduced by the exploits which still left their triumphant flush in his heart.

III

A YELLOW poster of the races stared out at him from the advertising column, and it occurred to him that at this hour Bogner must be at Freudenau, at the races; perhaps at this very minute he was engaged in winning the redemptory sum upon his own account. Was it credible that Bogner might remain silent about such a fortunate occurrence, and in addition, possess himself of the thousand gulden which Willi in the meantime would have won at cards from Consul Schnabel or Army Doctor Tugut? Why, certainly!—When one has once fallen so low as to take money from a stranger's drawer . . . And within a few months, perhaps even a few weeks, Bogner would be in precisely the same fix that he was in now. And then what?

Daybreak

Willi heard music. It was some Italian overture, in that half-forgotten style which is preserved only by these resort orchestras. But Willi knew this piece very well. Many years ago, he had heard his mother play it, four hands, with some distant relative. He himself had never been privileged to be his mother's partner at duet-playing; and when she had died, eight years ago, there were no more piano lessons, such as there had been before, when he had gone home from the military academy on his vacations. Softly and poignantly, the sounds rose on the tremulous spring air.

He crossed the little bridge over the muddy Schwechat and, after a few more steps, he reached the spacious terrace of the Café Schopf. It was always crowded on Sundays. Lieutenant Greising, looking pale and malicious, sat at a little table near the street. With him sat Wiess, the fat theatre manager, in a somewhat wrinkled, canary-yellow suit, with the eternal flower in his buttonhole. Willi had some difficulty in pushing his way among the tables and chairs to reach them.

"There is nobody here today!" he observed, extending his hand.

And he reflected with relief upon the possibility that the card game would not take place. But Greising explained that they two had merely been sitting in the open air, in order to recruit their energies for the "work." The others were already playing, inside. Consul Schnabel had arrived, having, as usual, come from Vienna in a fiacre.

Willi ordered an iced lemonade. Greising demanded to know where he had overheated himself, that he already needed a cooling drink, and remarked, with no further preliminaries, that the girls of Baden were decidedly pretty and temperamental. He then recounted, in not particularly choice phrases, the incidents of a trifling adventure which he had begun last evening in the park and which he had, that very night, brought to a successful conclu-

Daybreak

sion. Willi drank his lemonade slowly; and Greising, who noted the tenor of the latter's thoughts, responded with a little burst of laughter. "That," he said, "is the way of the world. You may take it, or you may leave it!"

Lieutenant Wimmer, of the Transport Corps (whom the unadvised often mistook for a cavalryman) suddenly appeared behind them.

"What do you say, gentlemen," he said. "Shall we worry ourselves to death, all alone here with the Consul?"

And he extended his hand to Willi, who, in his singularly conscientious way, although he was off duty, had saluted his ranking comrade.

"How are things going inside?" Greising asked, suspiciously and brusquely.

"Very slowly," replied Wimmer. "The Consul is sitting on his gold like a dragon—on my gold, at that. So up, gentlemen, and into battle, Toreadors!"

The others rose.

"I am invited elsewhere," Willi remarked, lighting a cigarette with feigned carelessness. "I shall just stay round for a quarter of an hour."

"Oh, come!" Wimmer laughed. "Hell is paved with good intentions."

"And Heaven with bad ones," added Wiess, the manager.

"Well said!" exclaimed Wimmer, and clapped him on the shoulder.

They went inside the coffee house. Willi glanced back regretfully over his shoulder out into the open, across the roofs of the villas, toward the hills. And he swore to himself that, in less than half an hour, he should be sitting in the Kessners' garden.

Together with the others, he entered a dark corner of the place, where the light and the spring air could not penetrate. In order to indicate that he had absolutely no intention of joining in the game, he had pulled his chair away from the table. The Consul, a lean gentleman of uncertain age, with a moustache trimmed in the English style and with reddish, partly grey, thin hair, immaculately clad in a light grey suit, was scrutinising, with his peculiar thoroughness, a card which Doctor Flegmann, the banker, had just dealt him. He won, and Doctor Flegmann drew some crisp, new notes from his wallet.

"Didn't bat an eye!" remarked Wimmer, with ironical appreciation.

"Batting one's eye won't alter accomplished facts," Flegmann answered calmly, his lids half closed. The Army Doctor Tugut, on detail in charge of the Military Hospital in Baden, laid down a bank of two hundred gulden.

The actor, Elrief, a young man from one of the leading theatres, but more celebrated for his parsimony than for his talent, allowed Willi to look at his cards. He risked small sums and, when he lost, shook his head, as if he were quite bewildered. Tugut soon doubled the capital of his bank. Wiess borrowed a small sum of money from Elrief, and Doctor Flegmann took more money out of his pocket. Tugut was on the point of withdrawing, when the Consul, without counting, cried: "Play the bank!" He lost and, with a swift glance into his wallet, he calculated his debt, which amounted to three hundred gulden. "Again!" he said. The Army Doctor refused. Doctor Flegmann took charge of the bank and dealt the cards. Willi declined to take a hand, but, purely in jest, "just to bring him luck," upon Elrief's continued pleading, he placed a gulden on the latter's card—and won. In the next deal, Doctor Flegmann tossed him a card, which he did not refuse. He won again, lost, won; he pulled his chair up to the table between the others, who very willingly made room for him, and won, lost, won, lost, as if Fate could not quite determine how she should conduct herself toward him today. Wiess had to leave to go to the theatre, and he neglected to repay his debt to Elrief, although he had already won back much more than enough. Willi was a little ahead

Daybreak

of the game, but he still lacked nine hundred and fifty gulden to make up the thousand which his friend so urgently required.

"There is nothing in this!" Greising insisted, dissatisfied.

The Consul took the bank again, and in a moment every one knew that the play was at last about to become serious.

Hardly anything was known of Consul Schnabel, except that he was the representative of a small free state in South America and a "wholesale merchant." It was Wiess who had introduced him into the officers' circle, and the manager's relationship with him originated in the circumstance that the Consul had known how to interest him in the engagement of a minor actress, who, immediately upon her appearance in a small part, had become very friendly with Elrief. The company would have enjoyed engaging in the good old custom of making sport of the deceived lover, but when the latter, his cigar between his teeth, would ask Elrief briefly, without looking up from the cards which he was dealing: "Well, how goes it with our mutual lady friend?" then it became clear that jests and sarcasm would be lost upon such a man. This impression was substantiated by a remark which he had made to Lieutenant Greising. Late one night, between two glasses of cognac, the latter had once indulged in certain offensive observations with regard to the Consuls of unknown countries. "Why do you stare at me, Lieutenant?" the Consul had replied. "Have you already made inquiries as to whether I am of a sufficiently high rank to give you satisfaction in a duel?"

A long silence followed this speech, and thereafter, as if by a tacit agreement, no further eventualities were risked, and it was unanimously decided, although by no concerted arrangement, that the Consul must be dealt with very carefully.

The Consul lost. No one objected when

he made a new bank after he had lost his first one, and, losing that as well, made up a third, although this was against the usual custom. The other players won, and especially Willi. He put his original capital, the hundred and twenty gulden, back into his pocket; these were not to be risked again, in any case. Then he laid down a bank himself. Soon he had doubled it. Then he withdrew, and, with a few aberrations, his luck held with him against the other bankers, who followed one another in quick succession. The sum of one thousand gulden which he had undertaken to win— for some one else—he had exceeded by several hundreds; and since Elrief had just risen to go to the theatre, to present himself for the rehearsal of a rôle of which he would say nothing despite the sarcastically inquisitive questions of Lieutenant Greising, Willi availed himself of the opportunity to accompany him. The others were soon deep in their play again; and when Willi turned to look at them as he reached the door, he saw that only the eye of the Consul had left the cards to follow him with a quick, cold glance.

IV

Not until he stood in the open air, with the sweet night breeze sweeping his brow, did Willi fully realise the enormity of his good fortune—or rather, as he immediately corrected himself, Bogner's luck. But even when Bogner had been provided for, he would have enough left over for himself to buy a new cape, a new cap and a new sword belt, just as he had dreamed. And in addition, a sufficient surplus for a few delightful suppers in some pleasant society, which would be easily found. And without counting the fact that he would have been plentifully compensated solely in being able to turn over to his old comrade, at half-past-eight upon the morrow, in front of the Alser Church, the sum required for his salvation. Here were a thousand gulden; yes, the celebrated golden thousand, which heretofore he had only read of in books, and which he now actually had in his wallet, together with several other one hundred gulden banknotes. Well, my dear Bogner, here they are. I have won these thousand gulden. To be absolutely precise, one thousand, one hundred and fifty-five. Then I stopped. Self-control, what? And I hope, my dear Bogner, from now on— No, no, he could not permit himself to preach. Bogner would himself adduce the necessary lesson; and it was to be expected that he would be sufficiently tactful not to make a precedent of this so happily terminated episode, and that he would not assume that he was now qualified to continue upon a friendly relationship with the Lieutenant. Still, it would perhaps be wiser, and even more correct, if he were to send his servant to the Alser Church.

On his way to the Kessners', Willi wondered if they would ask him to remain for

Daybreak

the evening meal. Well, fortunately, the meal itself was of no importance to him now. He was rich enough to take out the whole company, if he chose. It was a pity that there was no place where one could buy flowers. But he passed a confectionery shop which was open, and decided to buy a box of bonbons; and as he reached the door, he turned back to buy another, still larger box, reflecting how he should properly divide them between the mother and daughter.

When he entered the front garden of the Kessners', a housemaid met him with the information that the entire company had gone riding in Helenental. They had probably gone to Krainer Lodge. The company would no doubt dine out, as they generally did on Sunday evenings.

A mild disappointment was visible on Willi's face, and the maid smiled at the two boxes which the Lieutenant was holding in his hands. Now what should he do with these! "Please present my respects, and—

and please . . ." He extended the packages to the maid. "The larger one is for your mistress; the other, for the Fräulein. And say that I was very sorry."

"But perhaps, if the Lieutenant were to take a fiacre—the company is doubtless still at Krainer Lodge."

Willi looked at his watch, pensively and a little self-consciously.

"I'll see," he remarked carelessly, and, with a humorously exaggerated deep bow, he took his leave.

Now he stood alone in the evening street. A small company of happy tourists, ladies and gentlemen, with dusty shoes, passed by. In front of a villa, an old gentleman sat on a wicker chair, reading his newspaper. Further up the street, on a first floor balcony, an elderly lady sat crocheting, conversing the while with another lady in the house across the way, who was leaning out of an open window, resting her arms on the sill. To Willi, it seemed as if these few people were the only ones in the town who had not fled at this hour. The Kessners might have left some word for him with the housemaid! Well, he had no intention of intruding. There was really no occasion for that. But what should he do with himself? Should he go back to Vienna? Perhaps that would be best. But he would let Fate decide.

Two carriages stood before the casino. "How much to Helenental?" One of the drivers was already taken; the other one unblushingly demanded an exorbitant fee. So Willi decided in favour of an evening walk in the Park.

The Park was still quite crowded at this hour. There were married couples and pairs of lovers, which Willi had no difficulty in distinguishing apart. There were also young girls and women, walking alone or in twos and threes, who passed by him gaily. He encountered several smiling, even encouraging glances. But one could never be sure that there was not a father, a brother, or a fiancé walking behind, and an officer must needs be twice, nay, thrice careful. He followed a slender, dark-eyed lady, who was leading a boy by the hand. She ascended the steps of the terrace of the casino, seemingly looking for some one; at first, without result, until somebody eagerly beckoned to her from a distant table: whereupon she bestowed upon Willi a quick, triumphant glance, and joined the large company assembled there. Willi also looked round, as if he were expecting to find a friend; then he passed from the terrace into the restaurant, which was almost deserted, and went thence into the lobby, and then into the reading room, which was already lit up. There, at a long, green table, sat the solitary occupant, an old, pensioned General, in uniform. Willi saluted, bringing his heels smartly together. The General nodded with a bored expression, and Willi turned sharply round. Outside, in front of the casino, the unengaged fiacre was still waiting; and the coachman, unasked, declared himself willing to take the Lieutenant to Helenental.

"Thank you, but you are too late," Willi observed.

And, with rapid steps, he took himself off in the direction of the Café Schopf.

V

The players were still sitting there, just as they had been before, as if not a minute had passed since Willi's departure. The green-shaded electric light outlined the little group in a glare of livid brilliance. Consul Schnabel was the first to take any note of Willi's entrance, and Willi thought that he could detect a sarcastic smile on his lips. No one expressed the slightest surprise when Willi took his empty chair and pulled it forward again in its old place among the others. Doctor Flegmann, who was holding the bank, dealt him a card, as if it were the most natural thing in the world to do so. In his confusion, Willi put down a larger banknote than he had intended. He won, and proceeded more carefully. But his luck had changed, and soon there came a mo-

Daybreak

ment when his thousand gulden seemed to be in grave danger. What do I care? thought Willi; I shouldn't have had anything from it anyhow! But now he began to win again, and he did not find it necessary to change the bill. His luck remained with him, and at nine o'clock, when the game ended, Willi found himself in possession of two thousand gulden. A thousand for Bogner, a thousand for myself! he thought. Half of my portion I shall reserve as a gambling fund for next Sunday! But he did not feel as exultant as, in the nature of things, he ought to have been.

The entire company adjourned to the Stadt Wien for dinner. They sat under a shady oak in the garden and spoke about gambling in general, about famous card sessions played, for enormous stakes, at the Jockey Club. Flegmann, the lawyer, said, with great seriousness: "Gambling is, and will always be, a vice." Everybody laughed, and Lieutenant Wimmer diverted himself by extending the remark in a queer light.

That which was possibly a vice to lawyers, he observed, was far from being a vice to officers. Flegmann declared politely that one may be depraved and still remain a man of honour, and cited many examples, such as Don Juan and the Duc de Richelieu, to prove his contention. The Consul expressed the opinion that gambling was a vice only when one was not in a position to pay one's gambling debts. And in such cases, he added, it was not really a vice, but became a fraud, and a fraud of a particularly cowardly type. There was a moment of silence at this. But then, fortunately, Elrief appeared, with a flower in his buttonhole and with victory in his eyes.

"And did you fly so soon from the ovation?" Greising asked.

"I did not appear in the fourth act," the actor replied, and carelessly stripped off his gloves, as if he were rehearsing for the rôle of a Viscount or a Marquis.

Greising lit a cigar.

"It would be better for you if you did not smoke," Tugut observed.

"But, my dear Doctor!" Greising replied, "there's nothing the matter with my throat any more."

The Consul had ordered a couple of bottles of Hungarian wine. Toasts were drunk. Willi glanced at his watch.

"Oh, I'm so sorry!" he exclaimed. "I must go. The last train leaves at ten-forty."

"Finish your wine," said the Consul. "My carriage will take you to the train."

"Thank you, Sir, but I can't . . ."

"You can too!" Lieutenant Wimmer interrupted.

"Well, what do you say?" Doctor Tugut demanded. "Shall there be anything more doing tonight?"

No one had doubted that the session would be resumed after the evening meal. Such was the order of every Sunday. "But not for long," the Consul said. Lucky devils! thought Willi, and he envied them the prospect of sitting down at the card tables to try their luck once more, and possibly win thousands. The actor Elrief, whose wine invariably went promptly to his head, transmitted to the Consul a greeting from their mutual friend, Fräulein Rihoschek, smiling as he did so, with an inanely impudent expression on his face.

"Why didn't you bring the young lady along with you, while you were about it?" Greising demanded.

"She will come to the café in the evening, to spend a little time with us," Elrief replied. "That is," he added, mischievously, "that is, if the Consul will permit it!"

The Consul made no sign.

Willi finished his wine and rose from the table.

"Next Sunday!" Wimmer warned. "We shall take a little weight off you then!"

In that, thought Willi, you are mistaken, my fine fellow! There is no such thing as losing, if one is cautious!

"Will you be so kind, Lieutenant, as to send my coachman immediately back to the

Daybreak

café?" the Consul asked. And, turning to the others, he added: "But, gentlemen, we must not play so late, or rather, so early, as we did the last time!"

Willi once more saluted everybody in the circle, and turned to go. He was pleasantly surprised to see the Kessner family, with the corpulent lady and her two daughters, seated at an adjacent table. Neither the ironical lawyer nor the two elegant gentlemen who had arrived at the villa in the fiacre were present. The Lieutenant was joyfully greeted. He remained standing at the table, gay and unaffected, a chic young officer, in comfortable circumstances, not to mention the three glasses of strong Hungarian wine which he had imbibed, and, at the moment, without rivals. He was invited to sit down, but he declined, thanking them and excusing himself with a vague gesture toward the entrance, where the carriage awaited him. He was asked to answer one question: who was the handsome young man in civilian attire? Ah, an actor?

Elrief? Nobody knew the name. The theatre here, Frau Kessner asserted, was quite mediocre; there was not much more than operettas to be seen. And she continued, with a glance which encouraged delectable expectations, that, the next time the Lieutenant came, they might go together to visit the Arena.

"I think the nicest thing," Fräulein Kessner observed, "would be to take two boxes, next to one another."

And she smiled in the direction of Elrief, who smiled back at her.

Willi kissed the hands of all the ladies, saluted the officers at the next table once more, and, a minute later, he was sitting in the Consul's fiacre.

"Quickly!" he said to the driver. "You shall have a good tip."

Piqued by the indifference with which this promise was received, Willi reflected that the coachman was considerably deficient in respect. Still, the horses maintained an excellent pace, and in five minutes the station was reached. But at precisely the same moment, the train, which had arrived at the station a minute early, began to move. Willi leaped from the carriage, started after the lighted coaches as they began to move slowly and cumbrously over the viaduct, heard the whistle of the locomotive splinter in the night air, shook his head, and was not quite certain whether he was the more angry or pleased at his mishap. The coachman, perfectly unconcerned, sat on his high seat, stroking one of the horses with the handle of his whip.

"Well, I suppose there is nothing to be done about it!" Willi finally declared. And he turned to the coachman.

"Back to the Café Schopf!" he directed.

VI

It was pleasant to whirl through the town in a fiacre; but it would be more pleasant still, on such a mild summer evening, to be driving out into the country in the company of some attractive girl, and then to have supper, either in Rodaun or at the Rotan Stadt, out in the open. Ah, what bliss, not to have to gaze twice at every gulden before making up one's mind to spend it! Careful, Willi, careful, he said to himself; and he made a firm resolve on no account to risk all his winnings, but only half, at the most. And, moreover, he determined to employ Flegmann's system—to begin with small bets, not increasing until having won, and never to put the entire winnings back into play, but only three-fourths of the total amount, and so forth. Flegmann always began with this system, but he was never able to carry it through. So, of course, he got nowhere with it.

Willi swung himself down in front of the café, before the coach had quite stopped, and gave the driver a noble tip—so much that he might have hired a carriage for the amount. The coachman was still reserved, but his thanks were friendly enough.

The company was assembled to the last person, including the Consul's friend, Fräulein Mitzi Rihoschek—a stately little person, with excessively black eyebrows, but otherwise not too highly made up, and wearing a light summer frock, with a flat-brimmed straw hat with a red band on her brown, curly hair. Thus she sat next to the Consul, one arm thrown across the back of his chair, watching his cards. He did not glance up as Willi approached the table, yet the Lieutenant could feel that the Consul was at once aware of his presence.

"Missed your train!" Greising observed.

"Half a minute late!" Willi replied.

"Yes, that's how it goes!" Wimmer remarked, and dealt the cards.

Flegmann excused himself, since he had just lost three times running. Elrief was still looking on, although he had not a kreuzer left. A heap of bills lay in front of the Consul.

"There are big doings here!" thought Willi, and he put down ten gulden instead of the five which he had actually planned to risk. His boldness was rewarded. He won, and continued to win. Fräulein Rihoschek took a bottle of cognac from the sideboard, poured out a small glass for the Lieutenant, and handed it to him with an engaging smile. Elrief begged for the loan of fifty gulden, to be repaid the next day at twelve sharp. Willi passed him a note. An instant later, it had wandered over to the Consul. Elrief arose, perspiration standing out on his forehead. Attired in the glory of his yellow flannel suit, Weiss, the manager of the company, entered at this

Daybreak

moment and, after a low-toned conversation, was persuaded to repay the money which he had borrowed that afternoon. Elrief lost this also and, quite unlike the gallant Viscount whom he was accustomed to play on such occasions, he shoved back his chair in a rage, got up, muttering an oath, and left the room. When he did not come back after a certain time, Fräulein Rihoschek stroked the Consul's hair with a delicate and abstracted gesture, and left as well.

Wimmer and Greising, and even Tugut, had become careful as the end of the session approached; only the theatre manager still displayed some boldness. But gradually the game took the form of a duel between Lieutenant Kasda and Consul Schnabel. Willi's luck had shifted, and he had scarcely a hundred gulden left above the thousand reserved for his old comrade, Bogner. When these hundred are gone, I'll positively stop! he swore to himself. But he did not credit his own determination. What is this Bogner to me? he thought; I owe him nothing!

Fräulein Rihoschek reappeared, humming a melody. She stood before the big mirror and arranged her hair, lit a cigarette, took up a billiard cue and essayed a few shots, put the cue back in the corner, and amused herself by spinning alternately the white and the red balls on the green cloth. A cold glance from the Consul summoned her from this diversion. She began to hum again, took her place at his side, and rested her arm on the back of his chair. A student's song, shouted by a passing group of mixed voices, rose out of the silence outside. How are they going to get back to Vienna today? Willi wondered. And then it occurred to him that they might be students of the local gymnasium. Since Fräulein Rihoschek was sitting opposite him again, his luck was slowly returning. The song died out in the distance; a bell struck in a church tower.

"A quarter-to-one!" said Greising.

"The last bank," the Army Doctor declared.

"A bank all round?" Lieutenant Wimmer suggested. The Consul indicated his approval by a nod of his head.

Willi said not a word. He won, lost, drank a glass of cognac, won, lost, lit a fresh cigarette, won and lost. Tugut held the bank for a long time. The Consul finally relieved him of it with a high bet. Curiously enough, Elrief came back, after almost an hour's absence, and, still more curiously, he had money again. With a noble insouciance, as though nothing had occurred, he sat down, the living pattern of that Viscount whose rôle he would probably never play; and he had added a new attitude of superior indifference, which he had really copied from Doctor Flegmann, with his weary, half-closed eyes. He put down a bank of three hundred gulden, as if that were the most ordinary thing one could possibly do, and won. The Consul, without emotion, lost to him, to the Army Doctor, and especially to Willi, who was now the possessor of not less than three thousand gulden. That meant a new military cape, a new swordbelt, new linen, patent leather shoes, cigarettes, suppers for two and even three, rides in the Wiener Wald, and two months' leave of absence, in addition to the time due him! At two o'clock, he had won four thousand, two hundred gulden. There they lay before him; a concrete reality which could not be doubted—four thousand, two hundred gulden, and something over. The others had all fallen to the rear, and scarcely played any more.

"That is enough!" said Consul Schnabel abruptly.

Willi did not quite know how he felt. If they stopped now, then nothing more could happen to him, and that was well. At the same time, he was possessed of an uncontrollable, an absolutely fiendish desire to play on; to conjure a few more, or even all, of those crisp thousand gulden notes from

Daybreak

the Consul's wallet. That would be a capital with which one could make one's fortune! It did not necessarily always have to be baccarat—there were still such things as the horse-races at Freudenau and the Trabrennplatz, and there were gambling houses as fine as at Monte Carlo on the shore of the sea in the south. With beautiful women from Paris! . . . While his thoughts ran on, the Army Doctor was attempting to rouse the Consul to one last bank. Elrief acted as if he were the host, and served the cognac. He himself was drinking his eighth glass. Fräulein Rihoschek swayed her body and hummed a soundless melody. Tugut gathered the scattered cards and shuffled them. The Consul remained silent. Suddenly he called the waiter and ordered two fresh packs of cards. Everybody's eyes lit up. The Consul looked at his watch.

"At half-past-two," he said, "we shall stop. That is final!"

It was five minutes after two.

VII

The Consul put down a bank larger than any that this company had ever experienced—a bank of three thousand gulden. There was not a soul in the café, apart from the players and the single waiter. The morning songs of the birds drifted through the open door. The Consul lost, but he still maintained himself as banker. Elrief had completely recovered his losses, and a warning glance from Fräulein Rihoschek caused him to withdraw from the game. The others, who were all somewhat ahead, played modestly and carefully. Half of the bank still remained intact.

"Play the bank?" Willi suddenly proposed, and at once he was frightened at his own voice. Have I lost my mind? he thought. The Consul won, and Willi was

Daybreak

fifteen hundred gulden the poorer. Now, remembering Flegmann's system, Willi put down a ridiculously small sum, fifty gulden, and won. How stupid! he thought. I might have won the entire sum back in one trick! Why was I so cowardly?

"The bank, again!"

He lost.

"The bank, once more!"

The Consul seemed to hesitate.

"What has come over you, Kasda!" the Army Doctor cried.

Willi laughed, and felt the intoxication rising to his head. Was it the cognac which was dulling his reasoning faculty? Evidently! Of course he had made a mistake. He had had absolutely no intention of wagering a thousand or two thousand on a single play.

"I beg your pardon, Consul! I really meant——."

The Consul did not permit him to finish. He remarked, in an amicable tone: "If you did not know what sum was in the bank, of course I will take your retraction into consideration."

"What do you mean, take it into consideration, Consul?" Willi said. "A wager is a wager!"

Was it really himself that was speaking? His words? His voice? If he lost, then it was all over with the new cape, new sword belt, the suppers in the company of amiable women. There would remain, then, only the thousand for the defrauder, Bogner—and he himself would be the same poor devil that he had been two hours ago.

Without a word, the Consul uncovered his card—nine! No one uttered it aloud, yet it could be heard all over the room, in a kind of ghost-tone. Willi felt a strange moistness on his brow. God, that went quickly! At any rate, he still had a thousand gulden lying before him; in fact, a little more. He would not count it—that might bring him ill-luck. He was still richer than he had been upon leaving the train at noon. *Today* at noon? There was nothing to

Daybreak

compel him to risk the whole thousand at once. One might begin with a hundred, or with two hundred, Flegmann's system. Only, there was so little time left—hardly twenty minutes! Everybody was silent.

"Lieutenant?" the Consul began inquiringly.

"Certainly!" Willi laughed, and folded the thousand gulden note. "Half, Consul," he said.

"Five hundred?"

Willi nodded. The others also placed bets, but merely out of formality. The coming disruption was already apparent. Lieutenant Wimmer was standing up, with his cape round his shoulders. Tugut was leaning over the billiard table. The Consul uncovered his card—eight!—and half of Willi's thousand was gone.

He shook his head, as though there was something amiss.

"The rest," he said. I am really quite calm! he reflected. He uncovered his cards slowly. Eight! The Consul had to buy a card. Nine! And the five hundred were gone, the thousand were gone. Everything gone! Everything? No! He still had the hundred and twenty gulden with which he had come away in the morning, and even a little over that. Queer! Now he was suddenly only a poor devil, as he had been before. And the birds were singing outside . . . just as before . . . when he had been able to go to Monte Carlo. Well, it was a pity, but he had to stop now; these few gulden he certainly could not afford to risk. . . . He had to stop, although there was still a quarter of an hour remaining. What shameful luck! In a quarter of an hour, he might win five thousand, just as he had lost them.

"Lieutenant?" the Consul asked.

"I am very sorry," Willi replied, in a high-pitched, grating voice, and pointed to the few miserable bills laying before him. His eyes were actually laughing, and by way of a jest, he placed ten gulden on a card. He won. Then twenty. And won again.

Fifty—and won! The blood mounted to his head. He could have wept with rage. Now his luck had come—and it came too late! And with a sudden, bold resolve, he turned to the actor, who was standing behind him with Fräulein Rihoschek.

"Herr von Elrief, will you be so kind as to lend me two hundred gulden?"

"I am very sorry," Elrief replied, shrugging his shoulders with a noble gesture. "You yourself saw me lose everything, down to my last copper, Lieutenant."

It was a lie, and everybody knew it. But it seemed as if everybody thought it quite proper that the actor Elrief should lie to Willi. The Consul thrust a few notes across the table, seemingly without counting them. "Please help yourself," he said. The Army Doctor, Tugut, cleared his throat audibly. Wimmer warned: "In your place, Kasda, I should stop!" Willi hesitated.

"I don't wish to persuade you, Lieutenant," said Schnabel. He still held his hand spread lightly over the money.

Willi made a hasty movement toward the money, and then began to count it.

"There are fifteen hundred there," said the Consul; "You may be certain of it, Lieutenant. Do you want a card?"

Willi laughed.

"What else?"

"Your bet, Lieutenant?"

"Ah, not all of it!" Willi cried, his brain again becoming clear. "Poor folk must be economical! One thousand, to begin!"

He uncovered, imitating the Consul's habitual, exaggerated deliberation. Willi had to buy a card, and added a three of spades to his four of diamonds. The Consul also uncovered. He too held a seven.

"I should stop!" Lieutenant Wimmer warned once more, and now his words resounded almost as a command. And the Army Doctor added: "Now, when you are just about even—!" Even! Willi thought. He calls that even! A quarter of an hour ago, I was a well-to-do young man; now I am a pauper, and they call that "Even!"

Daybreak

Shall I tell them the story of Bogner? Perhaps they would understand!

There were new cards on the table. Seven! No, he did not wish to buy. The Consul did not even ask if he did; he simply uncovered his eight. A thousand lost—the figures buzzed in Willi's brain—but I shall win them back! And if I should not, it will not make any difference. I am just as incapable of paying back one thousand as two thousand. Nothing matters any more! Ten minutes still remain. I still have a chance of winning back all of the four, or even five thousand.

"Lieutenant?" the Consul inquired.

The room was full of reverberations, for every one was absolutely quiet, audibly quiet. And no one now ventured to say: I should stop, if I were you. No, Willi thought, no one dares to do that! They realize that it would be stupidity for me to stop now. But what sum ought he to wager? He had now only a few hundred gulden left. Suddenly he had more. The Consul had thrust two thousand more over to him.

"Help yourself, Lieutenant!" Assuredly, he helped himself! and put down fifteen hundred, and won. Now he could pay back his debt, and still have something left.

There was a hand on his shoulder.

"Kasda!" said Lieutenant Wimmer. "No more!" His voice was hard, almost severe. I am not on duty now, Willi remonstrated to himself, and outside the service, I can do what I wish with my money and my life. And this time he wagered modestly, only one thousand gulden, and uncovered his card. Eight. Schnabel still took his time, playing with funereal slowness, as if he had all the time in the world. There was still time; they were not obliged to stop at half-past-two. The last time, they had played till six. The last time . . . that beautiful, distant time. Why were they all standing round him? Just as in a dream. There, they were all more excited than he; even Fräulein Rihoschek, standing across from him, with her straw hat and its red band sur-

Daybreak

mounting her curly hair, had curiously shining eyes. He smiled at her. She had a face like the queen in a tragedy, although she was little better than a chorus girl. The Consul uncovered his cards. A queen! Ah, the Queen Rihoschek and a nine of spades! Damned spade! it always brought him ill-luck. And the thousand fared over to the Consul. Oh, that did not matter; he still had something left. Or was he completely ruined? Not at all! . . . Why, there were a few thousand again! Magnanimous Consul! To be sure, he was certain of getting them back. An officer had to pay his gambling debts. Such a person as Elrief remained Elrief in any case, but an officer, unless he happened to be called Bogner . . .

"Two thousand, Consul!"

"Two thousand?"

"That is correct, Consul!"

He did not buy a card; he held a seven. But the Consul had to buy. And this time, he did not bother to be ceremoniously slow; he was in haste, and added an eight—the eight of spades—to his one, which made nine. There was no doubt about that. Eight would have been sufficient, and the two thousand traveled back to the Consul, and thence back to Willi again. Or was there more than that? Three or four? It was best not to look; it brought ill-luck. The Consul would not cheat him; besides, everybody was standing round and watching closely. And since he did not know any longer just how much he owed, he put down two thousand again. The four of spades. Well, one had to buy to that; the six, six of spades. So that made one too many! The Consul did not have to trouble himself, and had only a three . . . and the two thousand wandered over, and wandered back again. Why, this was ridiculous! Forward and back. Back and forward. There! the clock in the tower struck—the half-hour. But no one gave any sign of having heard. The Consul dealt the cards quietly. Everybody was standing round; all the gentlemen, except the Army Doctor, who had disappeared. Yes, to be

Daybreak

sure! Willi had noticed, a little while ago, how he had shook his head with rage and mumbled something between his teeth. Doubtless he could not bear to look on, while Lieutenant Kasda was playing for his existence. Strange, that a doctor should have such feeble nerves!

There were cards in front of him again. He made his bet—he did not exactly know how much. A handful of bills. That was the new style: to let Fate take care of the amount. Eight! Now his luck had to change!

It did not change. The Consul uncovered nine, looked round the group, then pushed his cards away. Willi opened his eyes widely.

"What's up, Consul?"

The latter raised his finger and pointed toward the outside. "It has just struck the half hour, Lieutenant!"

"Really?" Willi cried, pretending astonishment. "Might not one play another quarter of an hour?" He looked round the circle, as if he sought approval. Every one was silent. Elrief looked away, in his most aristocratic manner, and lit a cigarette. Wimmer pressed his lips together. Greising nervously whistled an inaudible refrain. The manager, however, remarked, somewhat rudely, as if it were a small matter: "The Lieutenant has certainly had a run of bad luck tonight!"

The Consul had risen and called for the waiter, as though the night were like any other night. Only two bottles of cognac appeared on his bill, but, to simplify matters, he wished to take care of the entire check. Greising refused, and paid for his coffee and cigarettes. The others accepted his hospitality indifferently. Then the Consul turned to Willi, who had remained seated, and again pointed to the door, just as he had when he had verified the striking of the clock. "If you like, Lieutenant," he said, "I will take you back to Vienna in my carriage."

"That would be kind of you," Willi replied.

And at this moment, it seemed to him as if the last quarter hour, as if, in fact, the whole night, with all that had happened in it, had become inadmissible. The Consul apparently regarded it in the same light. Otherwise, how would he invite him into his carriage?

"Your debt, Lieutenant," the Consul added, in his most friendly manner, "amounts to exactly eleven thousand gulden."

"That is correct, Consul," Willi replied, with military briskness. "It will not be necessary to have it in writing, will it?"

"No," Lieutenant Wimmer interposed gruffly. "We are all witnesses!"

The Consul paid no attention either to him or to the tone of his voice. Willi still sat at the table. His legs had become as heavy as lead. Eleven thousand gulden! Not so bad! Approximately three or four years' salary, including bonuses. Wimmer and Greising were speaking together, in low, excited tones. Elrief was revealing something evidently very amusing to the theatre manager, since the latter burst into laughter. Fräulein Rihoschek stood near the Consul, and addressed a question to him in a low voice, which he answered in the negative, shaking his head. The waiter helped the Consul into his cape, a wide, black, armless cape with a velvet collar, which Willi had seen once before, and which had struck him as extremely elegant, though perhaps a little eccentric. The actor Elrief poured himself another glass of cognac from the almost empty bottle. It seemed to Willi that they were all avoiding him, as though they did not wish to be troubled with him, did not even wish to look at him. He rose with an abrupt effort. The Army Doctor, Tugut, who, most surprisingly, had returned, suddenly stood before him. At first he seemed unable to find words.

"I hope," he at last observed, "I hope, Lieutenant, that you are in a position to procure it by tomorrow morning?"

"Why, of course, Doctor!" Willi replied,

Daybreak

with a broad, vacant smile. Then he went over to Wimmer and Greising, and shook hands with them.

"Until next Sunday!" he said lightly.

They did not even answer; they did not even nod.

"Are you ready, Lieutenant?" the Consul asked.

"At your service!"

Now he took leave, in a very cordial and animated manner, of all the others; and, very gallantly, he kissed Fräulein Rihoschek's hand—it could do no harm!

Everybody left. On the terrace, the tables and chairs glowed a ghastly white; night still covered the city and the fields, though not a star was to be seen. In the direction of the station, the edge of the sky had begun to lighten. The Consul's carriage was waiting outside; the coachman was sleeping, his feet on the dashboard. Schnabel touched him on the shoulder. He awoke, raised his hat, shambled up to his horses, and took their blankets off. The officers touched their caps once more; then they sauntered away. The manager, Elrief, and Fräulein Rihoschek waited until the coachman was ready. Willi mused: Why does not the Consul stay in Baden with Fräulein Rihoschek? Why does he keep her, anyway, if he does not stay with her? It occurred to him that he had once heard a story of an old gentleman who had been struck with apoplexy while in bed with his mistress, and he glanced obliquely at the Consul. The latter, however, seemed both fresh and cheerful, not in the least ready for death; and it was patently in order to annoy Elrief that he took leave of Fräulein Rihoschek with delicate caresses, which somehow did not seem quite in accord with his usual disposition. Then he invited the Lieutenant into the carriage, offered him the place on the right side, spread a light yellow robe lined with brown plush over Willi and himself, and thus they drove off together. Elrief lifted his hat once more, with an elaborate, sweeping movement, not devoid of humour, according to the Spanish custom, just as he intended to do it at some little subsidized theatre during the next season, while enacting the rôle of a grandee. As the carriage wheeled round to cross the bridge, the Consul turned and waved a farewell to the three, who, arm in arm, with Fräulein Rihoschek in the middle, were just strolling away, and, engrossed in lively conversation, were not even aware of the Consul's parting gesture.

VIII

Not a sound was to be heard except the rhythm of the horses' clattering hoofs, as they rode through the sleeping city.

"It is rather cool," the Consul observed.

Willi had little desire for conversation; still, he realized the necessity of a reply, were it only in order to preserve the Consul's friendly attitude. So he said: "Yes, in the early hours of the morning it always freshens up a bit. We soldiers learn that in our encampments."

After a short pause, the Consul began, in a pleasant tone: "We need not be so exact about that matter of twenty-four hours."

Willi breathed more easily, and promptly availed himself of the opportunity which this remark afforded.

Daybreak

"I was just about to beg your indulgence, Consul," he said, "since, as you can well understand, I do not have the whole sum at hand at this very moment."

"Of course not!" the Consul interrupted. The hoof-beats rattled on, awakening echoes as they rode under a viaduct and out into the open country. "If I were to insist on the usual four-and-twenty hours," the Consul continued, "you would then be required to pay me your debt tomorrow evening, at half-past-two, at the latest. That would be inconvenient for both of us. Let us then set the hour"—he pretended to be considering the matter—"say, Tuesday at noon, at twelve exactly, if that suits you."

He extracted a visiting card from his wallet and handed it to Willi, who examined it attentively. The morning darkness had so far disappeared that he was able to read the address—Number 5, Helfersdorfer Strasse. Only five minutes' walk from the barracks, he reflected.

"Then tomorrow at twelve, Consul?" he

said, and he could feel his heart beating faster.

"Yes, Lieutenant, that is what I mean. Tuesday, at twelve sharp. I am in my office from nine o'clock on."

"And if I were not in a position to pay it at that hour, Consul—if, for instance, I could not satisfy you until the afternoon, or until Wednesday . . ."

The Consul interrupted him. "You shall certainly be in a position to pay your debt, Lieutenant. Since you sat down to play, you were naturally prepared to lose, just as I had to be prepared; and in the event that you did not dispose of a private fortune, you have, at any rate, no reason to fear that your parents will not support you!"

"I have no parents," Willi answered quickly, and Schnabel allowed a sympathetic "Oh!" to escape him. "My mother," he continued, "has been dead these eight years; my father, a Lieutenant-Colonel, died four years ago in Hungary."

"So your father was also an officer?" The

tone was sympathetic, actually warm-hearted.

"That is right, Consul. Who knows if I would have selected a military career, in other circumstances!"

"It is remarkable"—and the Consul nodded his head—"when you come to think of it, how some people's existence is, so to speak, planned out for them, while others don't know what they are going to do from one year to the next, sometimes not even from one day to the other! . . ." He paused and shook his head. This general, sober, unfinished sentence somehow struck Willi as reassuring. And, in order to make still more certain of this new relationship between himself and the Consul, he too attempted a somewhat generalizing philosophic phrase; and without reflection, as he was immediately aware, he remarked that there were officers, too, who were obliged to change their career, now and then.

"Yes," the Consul replied, "that is true; but that generally happens upon compulsion, and then they are, or at least, they feel themselves to be, ridiculously degraded, and it is usually not possible for them to go back to their former profession. On the other hand, such people as myself—I mean, people who, through no prejudice of birth, or rank, or anything else, are prevented—I, for example, have been at least half a dozen times above and below. And how far below!—ah, if you and your comrades knew how low I have been, it is hardly possible that you would have cared to sit with me at table. For that reason, you have all preferred not to make too careful inquiries concerning my position!"

Willi did not reply. He was very deeply touched, and not quite decided what attitude he ought to take. Of course, if Wimmer or Greising were here in his place, they would doubtless have found the right answer. But he, Willi, had to keep quiet. He did not dare to ask: What do you mean by "far below," and just what do you imply by "inquiries"? Oh, he could imagine

Daybreak

what was meant. He himself was now far below, as low as one could possibly be. Lower than, a few hours ago, he had imagined any one could be.

He was dependent on the Consul's state of disposition, on his willingness to meet him half way, on his mercy, however degraded socially he may once have been. But would he be merciful? That was the question! Would he consent to partial payments extending over a year—or over five years —or to a revenge match the next Sunday? He could not expect that—no, just at present he was not expecting that. And if he were not merciful!—well, there would be nothing left but to go begging to Uncle Robert. Still—Uncle Robert! It would be an extremely painful, actually a frightful resort, but none the less, it would have to be attempted. Absolutely! . . . And it was really unthinkable that his uncle would refuse to help him, when his career, his existence, his life—yes, to put it simply, the life of his nephew, the only son of his dead sister—depended upon his help. A man who lived on his income, who lived very modestly, but was nevertheless a capitalist, and who had merely to take the money out of the bank! Eleven thousand gulden! that wasn't one-tenth, not even one-twentieth of his fortune! In that case, it would be just as well if, instead of asking for eleven, he asked at once for twelve thousand gulden. And thus Bogner would likewise be saved. This thought put Willi in a more optimistic mood, somewhat as if he felt that Providence owed him a special consideration in recompense for his noble intention. But this was merely an alternative which he would keep in view, in the event the Consul was obdurate. And that still remained to be tested. Willi threw a quick glance sideways at his creditor. He seemed to be lost in memories. He had taken off his hat; his lips were half open, as if in a smile; he looked older and less severe than formerly. Was not this the right moment? But how should he begin! Confess frankly that one was simply not in a position—that one had let oneself into a situation without thinking—that one had lost one's head—in short, that, for a quarter of an hour, one had simply been incapable of lucid calculation? And, even then, would he have dared to go so far, would he have dared to forget himself so completely, if the Consul—there was no reason why he should not say so!—if the Consul had not, unasked, without even the slightest hint, placed the money at his disposal; in fact, passed it over to him; in a certain sense, forced it upon him, although in the most charming fashion possible?

"A ride like this, in the early morning, is quite marvelous, isn't it?" the Consul observed.

"Splendid!" the Lieutenant answered, sedulously.

"But what a pity," the Consul added, "that it always seems necessary to purchase such a ride by staying up all night, either gambling or doing something still more stupid!"

"As for myself," the Lieutenant observed eagerly, "it very frequently happens that I am up and in the open at this early hour, without having spent the night awake. The day before yesterday, for example, I was down in the courtyard of the barracks with my company at half-past-three. We drilled in the Prater. But, of course, I didn't ride down in a fiacre!"

The Consul laughed heartily, which raised Willi's spirits, although his gaiety had sounded somewhat forced.

"Why, I've occasionally had such experiences myself," the Consul said. "To be sure, not as an officer, nor even as an enlisted man—I never got that far. Imagine, Lieutenant, I did my three years' service long ago, and never rose beyond the rank of Corporal. I was such an uneducated person—at least, I was then! I have caught up a little during the passage of time; one gets the opportunity to do that on long voyages."

"I suppose you have seen a great deal of the world," Willi remarked obligingly.

"Indeed I have!" the Consul replied. "I have been almost everywhere—except to that country of which I am Consul. I have never been in Ecuador. But I have decided to drop my title of Consul very shortly, and to go away." He laughed, and Willi joined him, although a little wearily.

They were riding through a tedious, wretched district, among plain, drab, dilapidated houses. In a little front yard, an old man in his shirt-sleeves was watering the bushes; a young woman, in somewhat shabby clothing, stepped out into the street with a pail of milk purchased at an early opened shop. Willi felt a certain envy of these two, of the old man watering his little garden, of the woman who was bringing home milk to her husband and children. He knew that these two were happier than he. The carriage passed a high, bleak building, where a soldier walked up and down; he saluted the Lieutenant, who acknowledged the salute more politely than it was usual for one of his class to greet a common man from the ranks. The Consul looked long at this building, with an expression that was at once contemptuous and full of memories. This gave Willi something to think about. But how could it help him, at this particular moment, that in all probability the Consul's past had not been without stain? Gambling debts were gambling debts, and even a convicted criminal had the right to insist upon payment. Time was passing; the horses were going faster and faster, and in an hour, in half an hour, they would be in Vienna. And what then?

"And such creatures as, for example, your Lieutenant Greising, are permitted to go about at liberty!" the Consul said, as if in completion of a sequence of unuttered thoughts.

So I was right, Willi reflected. The man has been in prison! But at this moment, it does not matter. The Consul's remark implied a manifest insult to an absent comrade. Was that simply to be passed over, as though he had not heard it, or as though

Daybreak

he even agreed that the implication was just?

"I must beg you, Consul, to leave my comrade Greising out of the discussion!"

For this, the Consul had only a deprecatory gesture. "It's quite remarkable," he said, "how these gentlemen who are so severe in their professional honour, allow a man to remain in their midst who, with complete consciousness of what he does, endangers the health of another person; for example, a stupid, inexperienced girl, and thus sickens the creature, possibly kills her——"

"It is not known to us," Willi replied hoarsely. "In any case, it is not known to me."

"But, Lieutenant," the Consul said, "I had absolutely no intention of reproaching you. You personally are not responsible for these things, and it is not in your power to alter them."

Willi sought vainly for a reply. He reflected whether he was not in duty bound to report the observations of the Consul to his comrade—or ought he not, perhaps, talk the matter over thoroughly with Army Doctor Tugut? Or perhaps ask Lieutenant Wimmer for advice? But what had all this to do with him? His exigent concern was for himself, himself alone. His particular case—his career—his life! There, in the first beams of the sun, the monument of the Weaver at the Cross stood forth. And still he had not spoken a single word that was calculated to procure him an extension, even a short respite. Even as these thoughts flashed through his mind, he felt his companion's hand lightly touching his sleeve.

"I beg your pardon, Lieutenant," said the Consul, "Let us drop the subject! As a matter of fact, it ought not to trouble me if Lieutenant Greising, or anybody else, for that matter—all the more so, since I shall hardly have the pleasure of again sitting at the same table with these gentlemen."

Willi started.

"Just what do you mean, Consul?"

"I am leaving the country," the Consul answered calmly.

"So soon?"

"Yes, the day after tomorrow—more precisely, tomorrow—Tuesday!"

"Shall you be gone long, Consul?"

"Rather! From three to—thirty years."

The National Highway was already quite crowded with trucks and hucksters' wagons. Willi, whose head was bowed, saw the golden buttons of his cape glisten in the rays of the rising sun.

"Is this journey of yours the result of a recent decision?" he asked.

"Oh, not at all, Lieutenant! It was decided long ago. I am leaving for America. For the present, I am not going to Ecuador, but rather to Baltimore, where my family lives and where I also have a business. I haven't been there for eight years, and have not been able to supervise it personally."

So he has a family! Willi thought to himself. And how about Fräulein Rihoschek? Does she know that he is leaving? But what concern is that of mine! It's high time. I'm choking! And, involuntarily, he put his hand up to his throat.

"It is really most unfortunate," he said helplessly, "that you intend to leave tomorrow. For, you know, I was really expecting with some certainty"—he assumed a lighter, somewhat jocular tone—"that you would allow me the opportunity of a revenge next Sunday."

The Consul shrugged his shoulders, as though such a possibility were entirely out of the question. What shall I do now? Willi wondered. What shall I do? Shall I—beg him? Why should he be so insistent about a few thousand gulden? He has a family in America—and Fräulein Rihoschek! He has a business over there. What can these few thousand gulden mean to him? And to me, they are a matter of life and death!

They rode under the viaduct into the city. A train was just puffing out of the south station. There are people riding to Baden, Willi reflected, and further—to

Daybreak

Klagenfurt, to Trieste—and from thence, perhaps, over the sea to another hemisphere . . . and he envied all of them.

"Where shall I take you, Lieutenant?"

"Oh, please," Willi replied, "don't put yourself to any trouble! Drop me wherever it happens to be convenient for you. I live in the Alser Barracks."

"I will take you to the door, Lieutenant." He gave the coachman the necessary instructions.

"Thank you very much, Consul. It is really not necessary——"

The houses were all asleep. The street car tracks, still untouched by the day's traffic, ran along, smooth and gleaming, at their side. The Consul looked at his watch.

"We have made good time—an hour and ten minutes! Are you marching today, Lieutenant?"

"No," Willi replied, "Today I am to give classroom instruction."

"Well, in that case, you will be able to lie down for a while."

"So I shall, Consul, but I think I will take the day off. I shall report myself sick."

The Consul nodded his head, saying nothing.

"So you are leaving on Wednesday?"

"No, Lieutenant," The Consul replied, emphasizing every word, "tomorrow—Tuesday evening!"

"Consul, I must make a frank confession to you. It is extremely painful to me, but I am very much afraid that it will be wholly impossible for me, in such a short time—before tomorrow, at noon . . ." The Consul remained silent. He did not seem to be listening. "If you would be so kind as to give me a respite?" The Consul shook his head. "Oh, nothing very long," Willi continued, "and I might give you a confirmation or a promissory note, and I would engage upon my word of honour to find a way to settle it within two weeks . . ." The Consul still shook his head, mechanically, without any emotion. "Consul," Willi began again, and his voice, against his will, was pleading, "Consul, my uncle, Robert Wilram—perhaps you have heard of him?" The other continued to shake his head firmly. "You understand, I am not absolutely certain that my uncle, upon whom I can otherwise positively rely, will have this sum immediately at hand. But, of course, within a few days. . . . He is a rich man, my mother's only brother—a retired man, living on his income." And suddenly, with a queer catch in his voice which sounded like a laugh, he added: "It is really disastrous that you are going so far away as America, and so soon!"

"My destination, Lieutenant," the Consul replied calmly, "is a matter of absolutely no concern to you. It is common knowledge that debts of honour are to be paid within twenty-four hours!"

"I am aware of that, Consul, I am aware of that! Still, it happens now and then— among my comrades, I know many who, in a similar position. . . . It is entirely subject to your choice, Consul, whether you are willing to content yourself with a promissory note, or my word of honour, until—until next Sunday, at least."

"I shall not be satisfied, Lieutenant. Tomorrow, Tuesday, at noon—that's the limit of the period . . . otherwise, I shall report you to the commander of your regiment!"

The carriage went over the Ring and past the Volksgarten, whose rich, green foliage hung down over the gilded fence. It was a delightful spring morning. Hardly a person was as yet to be seen on the street; only a young and very elegant lady in a tailored suit was walking rapidly with her little dog, as if fulfilling a duty. She cast an indifferent glance toward the Consul, who turned round to look at her, in spite of his wife in America and Fräulein Rihoschek in Baden, who really belonged more to the actor, Elrief. What has Elrief to do with me, Willi said to himself, and why should I worry about Fräulein Rihoschek? Perhaps—who knows?—if I had been nicer to her, per-

Daybreak

haps she would have put in a good word for me! And for a moment, he seriously considered whether he ought not to ride back to Baden at once, to beg for her intercession. Intercession with the Consul? She would laugh at the idea. She knew the Consul too well; she must undoubtedly so know him. . . . And the sole possibility of deliverance was Uncle Robert. That much was certain. Nothing else was left beyond this, save a bullet in his temple. One was obliged to perceive that much very clearly.

A measured sound, like the approaching steps of a marching body of men, struck his ear. Was the 89th drilling today? On the Bisamberg? It would have been painful for him at that moment to be in a carriage and to meet his comrades at the head of their company. But it was not a military troop that was marching along; it was a group of boys, evidently school boys, who were going with their teacher on an outing. The teacher, a pale young man, looked with instinctive respect at the two gentlemen who were passing him in a carriage at this early hour. Willi had never fancied that he would live to know the moment when he would consider a poor school teacher as a being worthy of envy. Then the fiacre overtook the first street car, in which a couple of men in working clothes, and an old woman, were the only passengers. A street cleaning spray came towards them, on the top of which a wild looking fellow, with rolled-up sleeves, swung the hose like a rubber band. Two nuns, with lowered eyes, crossed the street in the direction of the Votive Church, which pointed its slender, light grey steeples to the sky. On a bench, under a tree covered with white blossoms, sat a young creature with dusty shoes, her straw hat in her lap, laughing as if after some agreeable experience. A closed carriage, with drawn curtains, whizzed past. And a fat old woman with a broom and a polishing cloth was cleaning the plate-glass windows of a coffee house.

All these people and things, which Willi

otherwise would not have noticed, now assumed a sharp and almost painful clarity in his wakeful eyes. And the man at whose side he was sitting had vanished from his mind. Now he looked at him again with a shy glance. The Consul was leaning back with closed eyes, his hat lying on the robe. How gentle, how kind-hearted he looks! And he—he was driving him to death! He was actually sleeping—or was he only pretending to be asleep? Don't worry, don't worry, Consul, I shall not importune you any more! You shall have your money, Tuesday, at twelve o'clock. Or perhaps not! But in no case . . . The carriage stopped before the gates of the barracks, and the Consul woke up at once—or pretended to have awakened at that very moment, and even went so far as to rub his eyes, with a gesture somewhat exaggerated to dispel a two and a half minutes' slumber. The guard at the door saluted. Willi leaped deftly from the carriage, without touching the running board, and smiled at the Consul. He even did something else; he gave the coachman a tip—not too much, not too little, like a cavalier, to whom losses or winnings meant nothing.

"Thank you very much, Consul—till we meet again!"

The Consul extended his hand from the carriage to Willi, as if he wished to confide to him something that everybody ought not to hear.

"I advise you, Lieutenant," he observed, in an almost paternal tone, "do not take this situation too lightly, if you place any value on your officer's commission! Tomorrow, Tuesday, at twelve o'clock!" Then, aloud: "Well, until later, Lieutenant!"

Willi smiled courteously, raised his hand to his cap, and the carriage turned and went off.

IX

The clock in the Alser tower struck a quarter-to-five. The big gate swung open. A company of the 89th, with eyes right, marched past Willi. Willi saluted several times, gratefully.

"Where are you going, Wieseltier?" he gently inquired of the last cadet.

"Rifle practice, Lieutenant."

Willi nodded, as if in agreement, and stopped for a moment to look at the receding company, although without seeing them. The guard still stood saluting as Willi passed through the gate, which was closed behind him.

He could hear sharp commands from the opposite end of the courtyard. A troop of recruits were practising the various rifle positions under the direction of a Corporal. The court lay in the glare of the sun, bare, except for a few trees scattered here and there. Willi walked along the wall; he looked up to his room, where his orderly had appeared at the window and, looking down, had stiffened for a moment in salute and disappeared. Willi hurried up the steps; he began to remove his clothes in the ante-room, where his orderly was lighting the little grate.

"At your service, Lieutenant! Coffee will soon be ready."

"Good," said Willi; and, going into his room, he closed the door behind him, took off his coat, and threw himself, in his trousers and shoes, on the bed.

I can't possibly reach Uncle Robert before nine o'clock. In any case, I shall ask him at once for twelve thousand, so Bogner will get his thousand, too, unless he has killed himself in the meanwhile. Anyhow, who knows? perhaps he really won at the races, and is even in a position to help me out! Nonsense! Eleven or twelve thousand gulden are not so easily won at the races!

His eyes closed. Nine of spades—ace of diamonds—king of hearts—eight of spades—ace of spades—jack of clubs—four of diamonds—thus the cards danced before him. His orderly brought in the coffee, pushed the table up to the bed, and poured; and Willi drank, reclining on one arm.

"Shall I take off your shoes, Lieutenant?"

Willi shook his head.

"It's no longer worth the trouble."

"Shall I wake you later, Sir?"—and, as Willi looked at him blankly—"Do you wish to report at the Academy at seven?"

Willi shook his head again.

"I am sick; I must go to see the doctor. Report me to the Captain . . . sick. You understand? I will send in the slip later. I have an appointment with an eye specialist at nine o'clock. Please ask the cadet-substitute, Brill, to take my place at the Academy. That is all. But wait!"

"Yes, Lieutenant?"

"At a quarter-to-eight, you will go over

to the Alser Church, and you will tell the gentleman who was here yesterday—yes, Lieutenant von Bogner, who will be waiting there—that he must be so kind as to excuse me—that, unfortunately, I was unable to do anything. Do you understand?"

"Right, Lieutenant!"

"Repeat!"

"The Lieutenant wishes to be excused; the Lieutenant was unable to arrange matters."

"Unfortunately, he was unable to accomplish anything. Wait! If there is still time before this evening or tomorrow morning"—he paused abruptly—"No, nothing more! I was unfortunately unable to accomplish anything, and that is all. Do you understand?"

"Right, Lieutenant."

"And when you come back from the Alser Church, be sure to knock. And now, close the window."

The orderly did as he was instructed, and a sharp command from the court below was cut short in the middle. When Joseph had closed the door behind him, Willi stretched himself out again, and his eyes closed. Ace of diamonds—seven of clubs—king of hearts—eight of diamonds—nine of spades—ten of spades—queen of hearts—damned canaille! Willi reflected. For the queen of hearts was really Fräulein Kessner. If I had not stopped at her table, the whole disaster would not have occurred. Nine of clubs—six of spades—five of spades—king of spades—king of hearts—king of clubs! "Don't take this matter too lightly, Lieutenant!" The devil take him, he will get his money! Then I shall send him two seconds!—It's a pity, but that will not do; he is not of rank! King of hearts—knave of spades—queen of diamonds—nine of diamonds—ace of spades! Thus they danced in procession before him—ace of diamonds—ace of hearts—irrelevantly, incessantly, until his eyes burned beneath their lids. There were certainly in the whole world not so many hands of cards as passed before his vision in this hour!

Some one was knocking. He woke up precipitately, the cards still passing before his open eyes. The orderly was standing before him.

"I wish to report, Lieutenant, that the Lieutenant thanks you many times for your trouble, and sends his respects."

"Is that all? He did not say more than that?"

"No, no, Sir! The Lieutenant turned round and left at once."

"Is that so! He left at once! . . . And you have reported me sick?"

"Right, Lieutenant!"

And, as Willi saw that his orderly was grinning, he asked: "What makes you laugh so stupidly?"

"Excuse me, Sir, it is because of the Captain!"

"Why, what do you mean? What did the Captain say?"

And the orderly explained, still grinning: "The Captain remarked that, if the

Lieutenant has to go to an eye doctor, he no doubt ruined his eyes looking at some girl!" And, when Willi did not smile, the orderly, becoming alarmed, added: "I felt that I ought to report what the Captain said!"

"You may go!" said Willi.

While he was preparing himself for the impending expedition, Willi revolved in his mind all manner of phrases, silently practising the tone which he should use, and by which he hoped to move his uncle's heart. He had not seen him for two years. At this moment, he was not able to visualize Wilram's bearing, nor even the lineaments of his countenance. The images which he brought to his mind were those of some one else, with different expressions, different manners, different ways of speaking; and he did not know which of these various images he was to meet. He had always thought of his uncle as a slender, rather fastidiously dressed, youthful man. Even in his boyhood, he had thought of him in that way, although, at that period, twenty-five years seemed to him a mature age. Robert Wilram had come to visit his brother-in-law, at that time still Major Kasda, for only a few days, in the Hungarian town where the latter was stationed on garrison duty. His father and his uncle had not appeared to get on very well together, and Willi retained a somewhat disquieting memory of one particular verbal encounter between these two, which had ended with his mother leaving the room, weeping. His uncle's profession had never come up in conversation, but Willi seemed to remember that he had once held some civil post, which he had given up when he became a widower. He had inherited a small fortune from his deceased wife, and since then, had lived on his income, traveling a great deal about the world. The news of his sister's death had reached him in Italy, and he had not arrived until after the burial; and in Willi's memory, there always remained the picture of his uncle standing at the grave, tearless, but with a desolated, grief-stricken expression, looking down at the still unfaded wreaths. Shortly after that, they both left the little city together—Robert Wilram to return to Vienna, and Willi to his cadet-school in Wiener-Neustadt. From this time on, his uncle had visited him occasionally on Sundays and holidays, taking him to the theatre or to a restaurant. Later, after his father's sudden death, and after Willi had been assigned as a Lieutenant to a Viennese regiment, his uncle, acting upon his own initiative, had allotted him a monthly allowance, which was paid at regular intervals through a bank when Wilram was absent on a journey.

Wilram had come back from one of these journeys, a completely altered man. He had been through a dangerous illness and, although the monthly allowance still came regularly, the personal relationship between the uncle and nephew suffered protracted interruptions, with occasional resumptions, which, in point of fact, formed the curious rhythm in the epochs of Robert Wilram's existence. There were periods when he lived a gay and social life, devoting himself entirely to the good things of the world; and then he would take his nephew to restaurants as before, and also to theatres, and to other pleasure resorts of a lighter character, upon which occasions there was usually also present some lively young lady, whom Willi then saw for the first, and indeed for the last, time. Then followed weeks during which his uncle seemed to have withdrawn himself entirely from the world and from people; and if Willi was admitted to his presence, he found a serious, laconic man, prematurely aged, who had wrapped himself in a dark brown dressing-gown resembling a clergyman's cassock, and who looked very much like a soured actor, as he strode up and down in his high-arched rooms in which the light never penetrated, or sat working beneath the electric light at his writing desk. The conversation usually dragged, as if the two were total strangers; upon a single occasion, however, when Willi chanced to mention a comrade of his who had killed himself in consequence of an unfortunate love affair, Robert Wilram had opened a drawer in his desk, and, to Willi's surprise, extracted a large number of manuscript pages, from which he read to his nephew some philosophic observations concerning death and immortality, and a number of other disapproving and melancholy remarks concerning women in general, during the course of which he seemed to have completely forgotten the presence of his nephew, who listened, a little embarrassed, and more than a little bored. Just as Willi was vainly endeavouring to stifle a yawn, his uncle happened to glance up from his papers. His lips curved into a vacant smile; he folded his papers together, put them back into the drawer, and immediately began to speak of other matters, which might be supposed to be of greater interest to an officer.

But even after this somewhat unfortunate meeting, there had still occurred a number of endurable evenings in the old manner; there were also some little walks together, especially on fine holiday afternoons. But one day, when Willi was to meet his uncle at the latter's home, he had received a message abruptly cancelling the appointment and, shortly thereafter, a letter explaining that Wilram was exceedingly busy at this time, and must beg Willi to cease his visits for the present. Soon afterwards, the allowance also ceased. A polite note, sent as a reminder, was unanswered. A second received the same fate. To a third, he received the reply that Robert Wilram was exceedingly sorry to be forced, "on account of fundamental changes in his situation," to cease further allowances "even to near relatives." Willi then sought a personal interview with his uncle. Twice he was not received, and on a third occasion, he saw his uncle disappearing through a door, at the moment when he had been told that he was not at home. The very small inheritance which had come from his mother, and which had sufficed him for his living expenses, had just been exhausted, but, up to this time, he had not given serious thought to the future. In his habitual fashion, he had neglected this detail until, suddenly, from day to day—yes, even from hour to hour—his difficulties had increased, and had gradually assumed threatening proportions.

Willi walked down the dark flight of steps. He was depressed, but not without hope. In the perpetual darkness of the spiral staircase, he did not immediately recognize the man who was barring his way.

"Willi!" It was Bogner addressing him.

"You?" What could he want? "Didn't you get my message? Did not Joseph tell you?"

"I know, I know! I only wanted to say to you—in case anything turns up—that the examination will not take place until tomorrow!"

Willi shrugged his shoulders. It really did not interest him very much.

"Postponed, do you understand!"

"That is not difficult to understand!" And he took another step down.

Bogner would not let him pass. "It is an omen!" he cried. "It means that I am going to be saved! Do not be angry, Kasda, that I have come again. I know, of course, that you had no luck yesterday——"

"You may be sure of that!" Willi exploded. "You may be sure that I had no luck!" And, with a burst of laughter, he added: "I lost everything—and a little more!" He could control himself no longer, as though he saw in Bogner the one and only cause of his misfortune. "Eleven thousand gulden, man! Eleven thousand gulden!"

"Good God, that is terrible! . . . What are you going to do?" Then he interrupted himself. Their eyes met, and Bogner's face lit up. "I suppose you will be compelled to go to your uncle now?"

Willi bit his lips. Pusher! Shameless! he

Daybreak

said to himself, and he was not far from saying it aloud.

"Pardon me!—It is none of my business—I mean, I ought not to interfere, all the more since I am, to a certain extent, the cause of it. Of course—! But if you are going to try it, Kasda—it might just as well be twelve thousand, instead of eleven thousand! It can't make much difference to your uncle!"

"You're crazy, Bogner! I have little enough chance of getting eleven thousand, let alone twelve thousand!"

"But you are going to try anyhow, Kasda!"

"I don't know——"

"Willi——"

"I do not know," he repeated impatiently. "Perhaps—and then again, perhaps not! . . . Good-bye!" He thrust him aside, and dashed down the steps.

Twelve or eleven, it was not at all a matter of no importance! A single thousand might break or make his chances! And the figures buzzed through his head: "Eleven, twelve—eleven, twelve—eleven, twelve! Well, he did not have to decide until he was actually in his uncle's presence. He would hear the answer at the proper moment. In any case, it was stupid of him to have told Bogner the sum, to have even allowed himself to be detained on the steps. What was wrong with the fellow? Yes, of course, they had been comrades, but never really friends! And now, was Fate to bind him and Bogner inextricably together? Nonsense! Eleven, twelve—eleven, twelve! Twelve had a better sound than eleven; perhaps it would bring him luck . . . perhaps a miracle would occur—if he asked for twelve, and not otherwise! And on the whole journey, from the barracks at Alser, through the city, to the ancient house in the narrow street behind the Cathedral of Saint Stephen, he considered whether he should ask his uncle for eleven or twelve thousand —as though success, and ultimately his life, depended upon his choice.

An elderly person, whom he did not know, answered his ring. Willi gave his name. He apologized for disturbing his uncle. Yes, he was really Herr Wilram's nephew! It was a matter of great urgency, and he would not take up much time. The woman was at first undecided; then she withdrew, and came back surprisingly quickly, with a more friendly expression, and Willi was admitted at once. He breathed freely again, and deeply.

X

His uncle was standing near one of two high windows. He was not wearing the clerical dressing-gown in which Willi had expected to find him, but had on instead a well-cut, although rather worn, light summer suit, with brown oxfords which had lost their gloss. With a remote and weary gesture, he motioned his nephew to approach.

"Glad to see you, Willi!" he said. "It is nice of you to think of dropping in on your uncle. I had thought that you had completely forgotten me!"

Willi was on the point of replying that he had not been received on his last visits and that his letters had not been answered, but he thought it best to express himself more affably.

"You live such a secluded existence," he said, "that I had no means of knowing if a visit from me would be agreeable to you."

The room was unchanged. There were papers and books on the writing table; the green curtain over the book-case had been half drawn aside, so that the same old leather-bound volumes were visible; the same Persian rug was spread over the divan, and the same embroidered cushions surmounted it. On the wall, there were two yellowed engravings, representing Italian landscapes, and there were family portraits in dull gold frames. His sister's picture stood, as formerly, on the desk. Willi recognized it from the rear, by its shape and the frame.

"Won't you sit down?" Robert Wilram asked.

Willi was standing with his cap in his hand, his sword at his side, stiffly erect, as if he were making an official report. In a voice which did not quite suit his posture, he began: "To tell you the truth, my dear

Uncle, I would not have come today either, if my business were not so extremely serious."

"You don't say so!" Wilram remarked, and his manner was friendly, but not particularly sympathetic.

"At least, it is very serious for me! In short, without beating about the bush, I have committed a stupidity, an enormous stupidity. I—I have gambled and lost more money than I possess!"

"Ah, that certainly is a little more serious than stupid!" his uncle observed.

"It was thoughtless," Willi agreed, "Criminally thoughtless! I don't wish to present it as any better than it is. But, remorse aside, my position is as follows: If I have not paid my debt by tomorrow at twelve, I am—I am simply—" He shrugged his shoulders, and stopped like a stubborn child.

Robert Wilram shook his head regretfully, but he made no reply. The silence in the room became at once so unbearable that

Willi was forced to speak. In rapid phrases, he told of the occurrences of the preceding day. He had gone to Baden, to visit a sick comrade; there he had met some other officers, old acquaintances, and had permitted himself to be drawn into a game, which had started innocently enough, but which developed, without his having anything to do with it, into a hectic affair. He would rather not reveal the names of those who had taken part, with the exception of the man who had become his creditor, a wholesale merchant, a South American Consul, a certain Herr Schnabel, who was unfortunately leaving at once for a long stay in America, and who had threatened to report him to the commander of his regiment, in case the sum were not immediately paid. "You know what that means, Uncle!" Willi concluded, and he sank exhausted on the divan.

Still his uncle did not look at him, but asked, in the same friendly voice: "How large is the sum in question?"

Willi hesitated again. First, he thought

of adding on the thousand for Bogner, and then he was suddenly convinced that this very addition might interfere with the outcome. So he asked only for the sum for which he himself was responsible.

"Eleven thousand gulden!" Robert Wilram repeated, shaking his head; and it sounded almost as if there was a tone of admiration in his voice.

"I know," Willi answered quickly, "it is a small fortune! And I do not seek to excuse myself. It was an act of unspeakable frivolity. I think it was the first, and I can assure you with certainty that it will be the last in my life. I can do no more than swear to you, Uncle, that I shall never again touch a card, as long as I live—that I shall exert myself, by a severe and scrupulous manner of living, to prove to you my eternal gratitude. I am even prepared—I swear it by all that I hold sacred—to forego all the claims which our relationship may have allowed to become established—for ever!—if only this time, just this once, Uncle——"

Robert Wilram had shown no emotion up to this point, but now he seemed to be affected to a certain degree. At first, he had raised one hand, as if to ward off his nephew's appeals; now he raised the other hand as well, as if he could silence him by this extremely expressive gesture; and, in a voice pitched unusually high, now almost mounting to shrillness, he interrupted him:

"I am very sorry! I am genuinely distressed, but, with the best intentions in the world, I cannot help you!" And, as Willi opened his mouth to reply, he added: "Absolutely, I am powerless to help you! It is useless to say anything more, so spare yourself the trouble!" And he turned toward the window.

At first, Willi was stricken, but upon consideration, he realized that he could not actually have expected to win over his uncle at the very first attack. And so he began again: "I am not deceiving myself, Uncle. I know that my request is an effrontery, a bit of unsurpassed impudence. And I should certainly never have dared to approach you, if there were even the slightest chance of getting the money in any other way. You must put yourself in my place, Uncle! Everything is at stake; not only my position as an officer! What should I do? How should I begin now? I have never studied anything; I don't know anything else. And I can't just go on living as a cashiered officer! Why, only yesterday, I chanced to meet a former comrade who, like myself— No, no! I would rather shoot myself! Don't be angry with me, Uncle. You must remember, Uncle, that my father was an officer; that my grandfather was a Lieutenant Field-Marshal when he died! For God's sake, I can't end it all in this way! That would be too enormous a punishment for a foolish prank! I am not a hardened gambler. You know that. I have never gotten into debt. Not even in the last year, when I often had great difficulty in getting through. And I never allow myself to be tempted, although I might do so very often.

Daybreak

Of course, it is quite a large sum! I don't believe I could get such an amount from a usurer. And what would happen if I could? In half a year, I should owe twice as much; at the end of a year, ten times—and——"

"Enough, Willi!" Wilram interrupted him in a still shriller voice. "That is enough! I can't help you! I wish I could, but I cannot! Don't you understand? I myself have nothing! I haven't even a hundred gulden in all, as I stand here before you! There, there! . . . " He pulled out, one after another, the drawers of the dressing table, as if these were witnesses to the truth of his words, since there were no notes or coins to be seen, but only papers and boxes and linen, of every description. Then he tossed his purse on the table. "You can look for yourself, Willi, and if you can find more than a hundred gulden, then you may hold me responsible for whatever you wish!" And he sank suddenly into the desk chair and let his arms fall on the surface of the table, so heavily that some sheets of paper fluttered to the ground.

Willi picked them up carefully, and then he looked round the room, as if he thought that he might discover some change which would help him to understand the inconceivably altered circumstances of his uncle. But everything was just as it had been two or three years before. And he asked himself if conditions were really as his uncle had represented them. Was not this extraordinary old man, who had so suddenly left him stranded two years earlier, capable of prevarication, of enacting a comedy fabricated for the purpose of rendering his refusal realistic and of securing himself against the continued importunities of his nephew? Was all that he claimed possible? How could one who, as he himself stated, possessed nothing, live in such a well-ordered house, in the central part of the city, and keep a housekeeper? The beautiful leather bindings still filled the bookcases; the pictures framed in dull gold still hung on the walls—and the owner of all these treasures had meanwhile become a beggar? What had he done with all his fortune, in the past two or three years? Willi did not believe him, and he had not the slightest reason to believe him, and still less cause to confess himself beaten, since, in any case, he had nothing more to lose. Consequently, he determined to make a last attempt, which did not turn out to be as bold as he had planned; for, to his own surprise and shame, he suddenly found himself standing before his Uncle Robert, with clasped hands, and pleading: "It is a matter of my life. My life is at stake. I beg you. I—" His voice failed him and, following a sudden inspiration, he grasped the photograph of his mother and held it before his uncle, as if he were adjuring him on her behalf. The latter, however, merely wrinkled his brow, gently removed the picture from his hand, and calmly put it back in its place.

"Your mother has nothing to do with the

case," he remarked, in a low, but by no means angry voice. "She cannot help you any more than I can. If I did not really wish to help you, Willi, I should not need any excuses. I do not recognize any duties, especially in such a situation as this. And, in my opinion, one can still be a very honourable man—even in civilian life! Honour is lost in other ways. You have not reached the point where you can understand that. Therefore, I tell you again, if I had the money, you may be certain that I would give it to you. But I have nothing. I have nothing at all! I no longer possess a fortune. I have only an annuity. Yes, on the first and the fifteenth of every month, I get exactly so much, and today"—he pointed to the purse with a lugubrious smile—"today is the twenty-seventh!" Then, observing in Willi's eyes a sudden gleam of hope, he immediately added: "And you fancy that I could make a loan on the strength of my annuity? But, my dear Willi, such an arrangement is entirely dependent upon the circumstances under which one has procured his annuity!"

"Perhaps, Uncle, perhaps it might still be possible! Perhaps we two together——"

Robert Wilram interrupted him furiously. "Nothing is possible! Absolutely nothing!" And, as though in the deepest despair: "I can't help you! Believe me, I cannot!"—and he turned away.

Willi reflected briefly. Then he spoke. "Well, there is nothing to be done, then, but to beg your pardon for having thus— good-bye!"

He had already reached the door when Robert's voice stopped him. "Willi, come here! I don't want you to judge me harshly. I must explain to you. You must understand that I have turned over my entire fortune, or rather, what remained of it, to my wife!"

"You are married!" Willi cried in astonishment, and a new hope rose in his eyes. "Then, if your wife has the money, a way out ought certainly to be found. I mean, if you were to tell your wife that it is a matter——"

Robert Wilram interrupted him with an impatient gesture. "I shall tell her nothing. Don't urge me any further. It would be useless!" He was silent.

But Willi, unwilling to relinquish this last hope so quickly, sought to press the subject. "I suppose," he said, "your wife does not live in Vienna?"

"Oh, yes, she lives in Vienna, but not with me, as you may perceive." Wilram strode up and down the room, and then, with a bitter laugh, he said: "Yes, I have lost more than a sword belt, and you see that I am still alive! Yes, Willi—" He stopped suddenly, and then began again: "A year and a half ago, I turned over my entire fortune to her, of my own free will. And I did it really as much for my own sake as for hers . . . for I am not very domestic nor economical, and she—she is very thrifty, one must admit that, and very business-like, and she has invested the money most wisely.

Better than I had ever managed it. She invested it in some kind of enterprise—I have not been apprised of the exact circumstances—I would not understand it anyhow! And the income which I receive amounts to twelve and one-half percent. That is not so meagre, and I have no right to complain . . . twelve and one-half percent. And not a kreuzer more! And every attempt that I made in the beginning to get an occasional advance was in vain. After the second attempt, I very wisely gave up trying. For I subsequently was not allowed to see her for six weeks, and she swore that I should never see her again, if I ever came to her with any such requests. And I have never cared to take that risk. I need her very badly, Willi; I can't exist without her! Every week I see her. She comes to me once a week. Yes, she holds to our agreement! She is really the most punctual creature in the world. She has never failed to come, and the money has always come promptly on the first and the fifteenth. And in the summer, every year, we go together to the country for two weeks. That is also in our contract. And the rest of the time is her own."

"And you yourself, Uncle, do you never visit her?" Willi asked, somewhat confused.

"Why, of course, Willi! Every Christmas day, every Easter Sunday, and every Whitmonday! That comes on the eighth of June, this year."

"Pardon me, Uncle, but what if it should occur to you to go to visit her on some other day? Why, after all, you are her husband, and who knows but that it might rather flatter her, if sometimes——"

"I dare not risk it!" Robert Wilram interrupted. "Once—since I have told you so much, I may as well tell you this!—well, once I walked up and down in front of her house, in the evening, for two hours——"

"And what happened?"

"She did not show herself. But the next day, I received a note from her which con-

Daybreak

tained only these words, that I should never in her life see her again, if I ever again took a notion of promenading up and down before her house. Yes, Willi, that is the way it is! And I know that if my own life depended on it, she would see me die before she would pay me even a tenth of what you ask, before it became due. You stand a much better chance of persuading the Consul to have clemency than I have of persuading my wife."

"And—was she always that way?" Willi asked.

"That has nothing to do with the matter," Robert Wilram replied impatiently. "Even if I had foreseen everything, it would not have helped matters. I was doomed from the moment I laid my eyes on her; at least, from our first night on—and that was our wedding night!"

"Of course!" Willi said, as if to himself.

Robert Wilram burst into laughter. "Oh, you imagine that she is a young lady from a good, respectable home? Far from it, my dear Willi! She was a prostitute. And who knows if she is not one still—for others!"

Willi felt called upon to express his doubt through some gesture; and he really entertained a doubt, for after his uncle's story, it was impossible to imagine this prodigious woman as a young and charming creature. Throughout his uncle's recital, he had thought of her as a spare, yellow, inelegantly dressed, elderly person, with a sharp nose, and he wondered hastily if his uncle were not inclined to revenge himself for her shameful treatment of him by calling her undeserved names. But Robert Wilram cut short his thoughts by continuing. "Well, prostitute is perhaps a little too severe—in those days, she was really a flower girl. I met her at Hornig's. I saw her there, for the first time, four or five years ago. You were with me. You might perhaps recall her." And, encountering Willi's questioning look, he continued: "We were there among a large company. It was a banquet for the singer, Kriebaum. She wore

Daybreak

a bright red dress, and she had wild, blond hair, and a blue ribbon round her neck." And he added, with a kind of suppressed joy: "She looked quite different. She was able to take her pick of men then. Unfortunately, I never had any luck with her. In other words, I was not worth her trouble, on account of my age. And then it happened, just as it always happens when an old fool goes mad over a young girl! So, two and a half years ago, I married Fräulein Leopoldine Lebus."

So her name was Lebus, Willi thought. For Willi at once remembered, although he had long since forgotten the episode, that this was none other than his own Leopoldine. He was certain of it, as soon as his uncle mentioned Hornig's, the red dress, and the wild, blond hair. Naturally, he did not tell his uncle how that evening at Hornig's had ended. For, although his uncle cherished no illusions concerning Leopoldine's past life, it would doubtless have pained him a great deal to have learned that, after he had accompanied his uncle home, Willi had secretly met Leopoldine again and stayed with her until the next morning. So to prevent this, he pretended that he could not quite remember the occasion; and he remarked, as if thereby to console his uncle, that such wild blondes sometimes made very fine wives and housekeepers, whereas, on the contrary, girls with excellent reputations and coming from good families often gave their husbands terrible surprises. He had observed an example in the case of a certain baroness, who had married a comrade of his. She was a young lady from one of the finest aristocratic houses, and another of his comrades had been presented to her, not two years after the marriage, in a "salon" where "respectable women" were to be had at stipulated prices. The unmarried comrade had felt himself obliged to reveal this circumstance to the husband. The result—a court of honour, a duel, the severe wounding of the husband, the suicide of the wife. Uncle Robert must have read about it in the papers, there had been so much talk about the matter. Willi spoke with animation, as if this affair interested him more than his own, and Robert Wilram began to look at him more amiably. Willi was thinking rapidly, and he had decided upon a sudden, bold coup; and, although his uncle could not possibly suspect it, he judged it wiser to lower his voice and to abandon the subject which did not rightly belong to the situation before him. And, without transition, he declared that, after the revelations which his uncle had made, he would certainly not urge him further, and he even allowed his uncle to believe that it was better to attempt to persuade Consul Schnabel than the former Fräulein Leopoldine Lebus. Moreover, it was not at all inconceivable that Lieutenant Hoechster, who had inherited some money, and a certain Army Doctor, who had taken part in the game, would co-operate to help him out of his dreadful situation. He ought to go to see Hoechster at once. He was on duty at the barracks today.

Willi looked at his watch. His feet were itching to depart, and, suddenly declaring that there was no time to be lost, he shook hands with his uncle, tightened his sword belt, and left.

XI

The first thing to be done was to discover Leopoldine's address, and that without loss of time. Willi went directly to the registration office. That they might refuse his request, he could not at the moment believe, especially if he were to convince them that his life depended upon it. Her image, which had not come to his mind in all these years, suddenly rose clear and distinct before him, together with the memory of all the other events of that evening. Again he saw her blond head lying on the rough linen pillowcase, through which the red pillow beneath shimmered like a blush. He remembered her pale, childlike face, striped by the split rays of the morning sun that pierced the latticed window, saw again her arm stretching out from beneath the covers to bid him good-bye, and recalled a gold ring with a semi-precious stone, and a slender silver bracelet. She had pleased him so well that he was firmly decided, when he had left her, that he should see her again. It happened, however, that at that time another woman had previous claims on him, one who, being kept by a banker, never cost him a kreuzer—which, in his position, was a point in her favour which was not to be lightly considered; and thus it chanced that he had never gone to Hornig's again, and had never made use of the address of Leopoldine's married sister, with whom she lived, and where he might have written to her. Thus, he had never seen her again, after that single night. Still, however vastly her life may have changed since that time, she could not possibly have so greatly altered that she would stand by and see happen—what had to happen, should she refuse his so easily satisfied plea.

He was obliged to wait an hour at the registration office before they gave him her

Daybreak

address on a slip of paper. Then he took a closed carriage to the corner of the street where Leopoldine lived, and got out.

It was a new house, four stories high, of a not very prepossessing appearance, situated directly opposite a lumber yard. On the second floor, a neatly garbed maid opened the door for him. At his question, whether Frau Wilram was at home, she looked at him hesitatingly, whereupon he handed her his visiting card—Wilhelm Kasda, Lieutenant in the 89th Imperial and Royal Regiment of Infantry, Alser Barracks. The maid came back at once with the answer that Frau Wilram was very busy —what did the Lieutenant desire? And then only did it occur to him that Leopoldine did not know his last name. He was wondering whether he ought to present himself simply as an old friend, or jocularly as a cousin of Herr von Hornig, when the door opened and an old, poorly dressed man with a black brief case emerged and walked toward the outer door. Then a woman's voice called out: "Herr Krassny!" but the latter did not seem to hear, for he was already descending the steps. Then the lady herself came into the hall and called again to Herr Krassny, so that this time he turned round. Leopoldine had already noticed the Lieutenant, and had recognized him at once, as her glance and her smile disclosed. She was not at all the same creature as his mind's eye had recalled. She was better poised and of a fuller figure; she even appeared to be taller, and she wore her hair in a flat, severe coiffure. And—this was the most surprising thing of all—a golden pince-nez surmounted the piquancy of her tiny nose.

"How do you do, Lieutenant?" she said, and for the first time he noticed that her features were really quite unchanged. "Please go right in. I'll be ready in a moment." She pointed to the door whence she had come, turned to Herr Krassny, and seemed to be admonishing him very particularly with regard to some commission, but in a voice so low that Willi could not understand what she said. Meanwhile, Willi entered a large, light room, in the centre of which stood a long table with pens and ink, pencils, a ruler, and ledgers; along the walls, to the right and to the left, were two high filing cabinets; on the rear wall, over a table covered with newspapers and prospectuses, hung a huge map of Europe: and Willi was unconsciously reminded of a traveler's agency in a provincial city, where he had once transacted some business. And a moment later, he remembered the poor hotel room, with its dilapidated lattice and the worn pillowcase —and he had a strange sensation, as if he were dreaming.

Leopoldine entered, closing the door behind her. She took off her eye-glasses and toyed with them for a moment; then she extended her hand to the Lieutenant, in a friendly enough manner, but with a complete absence of enthusiasm. He bent over her hand, as if he were about to kiss it, but she withdrew it at once.

"Won't you sit down, Lieutenant? To what do I owe this pleasure?" She pointed to a comfortable armchair, while she herself took her apparently customary place in a straight-backed chair opposite the long table with the ledgers. Willi had the impression that he was in the office of a lawyer or a physician. "What can I do for you?" she asked, and her voice, which was almost impatient, did not sound very encouraging.

"In the first place," Willi began, clearing his throat in embarrassment, "I must say it was not my uncle who gave me your address!"

Leopoldine looked up in astonishment.

"Your uncle?"

"My uncle, Robert Wilram!" Willi replied, with emphasis.

"Oh, of course!" She smiled and looked down.

"He knows absolutely nothing of this

visit," Willi continued rapidly. "I want to make that very plain." And, at her astonished glance, he added: "I really had not seen him for a very long time, but that was not my fault. Only today, in the course of our conversation, he revealed to me the fact that, in the meanwhile, he had—married."

Leopoldine nodded her head. "A cigarette, Lieutenant?" She indicated an open box. He took a cigarette; she struck him a match, and also lit one for herself. "Very well! And may I now finally know to what circumstance I am indebted for the pleasure of this visit?"

"It has to do with the same business which led me to visit my uncle. A rather unpleasant affair, as I am sorry I have to admit at once!" And he continued, as her expression grew severe: "I don't wish to take up too much of your time. So, without further preliminaries, let me say that I should like to have a certain sum advanced to me, for a period of three months!"

Her expression at once became surprisingly amiable. "Your confidence is extremely flattering, Lieutenant!"—and she brushed the ashes off her cigarette—"although I really can't imagine why you should honour me in this way! However, may I ask what the amount would be?" And she drummed lightly upon the table with the edge of her pince-nez.

"Eleven thousand gulden, Madam!" He was sorry he had not said twelve. He was about to correct himself, when it suddenly occurred to him that the Consul would be satisfied with ten thousand, and in that case, he would have enough with eleven.

"Ah!" Leopoldine exclaimed. "Eleven thousand! Eleven thousand! That really is quite a considerable sum!" Her tongue played against her teeth. "And what security can you offer me, Lieutenant?"

"I am an officer, Madam!"

She smiled, almost gently. "I beg your pardon, Lieutenant, but, in business practice, that is hardly sufficient as security. Who would be willing to answer for you?"

Daybreak

Willi remained silent and gazed at his shoes. A curt refusal could not have embarrassed him more than this cold politeness.

"And I beg *your* pardon, Madam!" he replied. "I have not, I admit, sufficiently considered the formal side of the situation. As it happens, I am in a desperate position. It concerns a debt of honour, which must by all means be settled tomorrow: for otherwise, my honour shall be forfeited, and in addition—that which, among us officers, must not be kept when honour has been lost!" And, fancying that he saw a gleam of sympathy in her eyes, he related, just as he had related to his uncle an hour before, but using more elegant and lively phrases, the story of the preceding night. She listened to him with visibly increasing signs of sympathy, even of pity; and when he had ended, she asked, with promise shining in her eyes: "And I—I, Willi! Am I the only person on earth to whom you can go in this emergency?"

These words, and especially her use of the familiar form, encouraged him. Already he believed himself saved. "Would I be here, if it were otherwise?" he asked. "I have really no one else!"

She shook her head sympathetically. "That makes it all the more painful," she replied—slowly, she extinguished her glowing cigarette—"for I am really not able to help you. My money is invested in various enterprises. I never have access to large sums of cash. I am really very sorry!" And she rose from her chair, as if to bring the interview to an end. Willi, terribly frightened, remained seated, and hesitatingly, clumsily, almost stutteringly, he suggested that there might possibly be some hope of securing a loan from some bank, or that some credit might be at her disposal in view of the excellent condition of her commercial enterprises. Her lips curved ironically, and she smiled indulgently at his ingenuousness.

"You imagine that these things are much

more simple than they are," she said, "and apparently you take it quite for granted that I should undertake, in your interests, a financial transaction which I should never think of resorting to in my own! And, in addition to that, without any security! Your assurance astounds me!" These last words were spoken in a tone so cordial, even so coquettish, that it seemed to Willi that in her heart she was already prepared to yield, and was only waiting for a beseeching word upon his part. He thought that he had found it, and exclaimed: "Madam!—Leopoldine!—My existence, my life is at stake!"

She started, and, fearing that he had ventured too far, he added softly: "I beg your pardon!"

Her eyes became impenetrable, and, after a short silence, she remarked shortly: "In any case, I can't make a decision until I have consulted my lawyer." Then, as his eye gleamed with resurrected hope, she made an evasive gesture: "I had an appointment with him anyhow—for today, at five o'clock, in his office. I will see what can be done. However, I should advise you not to depend on it at all. For I have no intention of making it a question of vital importance!" And, with a sudden hardness, she added: "I don't really know why I should!" But then she smiled again, and gave him her hand. And this time she even permitted him to kiss it.

"When may I come for my answer?"

She seemed to be considering for a moment. "Where do you live?" she asked.

"Alser Barracks," he answered promptly. "Officer's wing, third floor, room four!"

She smiled vaguely; then she said, slowly: "At seven, at half-past seven, at the latest, I shall know whether or not I shall be able . . ." She reflected again for a moment, and then finished decisively: "I shall send you my answer between seven and eight, by a person whom I can trust." She opened the door for him, and accompanied him into the hall. "Good-bye, Lieutenant!"

"Till we meet again!" he amended, somewhat taken aback. Her expression remained cold and distant. And when the maid opened the door to the staircase for Willi, Frau Leopoldine Wilram had already disappeared into her room.

XII

During the short time that Willi had remained with Leopoldine, he had traversed so many changing emotions of despair, of hope, of security, of renewed disappointment, that he felt, as he descended the staircase, as if he had lost his mind. But, when he had come again into the open air, his brain cleared, and now it seemed to him, upon reflection, that, on the whole, his condition was not unfavourable. It was certain that, if she but wished to do so, Leopoldine was perfectly able to procure the money for him. Her entire attitude had made it clear to him that it was in her power to influence her attorney as she pleased. And in particular, the feeling that there was still something remaining in her heart which pleaded for him, so powerfully

Daybreak

intoxicated Willi that in his mind he jumped the intervening interval, and contemplated himself suddenly as the husband of the widow, Frau Leopoldine Wilram, now Frau Major Kasda.

But this dream-picture soon faded as he walked aimlessly in the midday heat through the slightly crowded streets, in the direction of the Ring. He remembered again the disagreeable office room in which she had received him, and her aspect, which for a while had been graced by a certain womanly spirit, but which had then taken on the hard, almost severe expression which, from time to time, had intimidated him. There were still a great many hours of uncertainty before him; and no matter what the result was to be, these had to be passed in some manner. He conceived the fancy of having a good time, even if it were to be his last. Precisely because it was to be his last! He determined to have luncheon in an aristocratic hotel restaurant, where he had gone occasionally with his uncle. He selected a table in a cool, quiet corner, ordered an excellent meal, drank a bottle of dry, sweet Hungarian wine, and soon found himself in such a placid mood that even the thought of his lamentable situation could not disturb it. He sat for a long time, now the solitary guest, smoking a good cigar in the corner of a velvet couch, and felt half giddy, half sleepy. When the waiter offered him imported Egyptian cigarettes, he purchased a whole box at once. What did it matter? At the worst, his orderly would inherit them.

When he passed again into the street, his mood was no different than if he had been involved in a somewhat serious, but in the main rather interesting adventure; as if he were anticipating a duel. And he remembered half a night which he had passed, two years before, with a comrade who was to fight with pistols the next morning. Earlier in the evening, they had enjoyed the company of a couple of young ladies; then, when they were alone, they had had a serious and somewhat philosophical discussion.

Yes, his mood then must have been the same. And since that affair had turned out well, it seemed to Willi a favourable omen.

He sauntered through the Ring—a young, not overly elegant officer, but of good, slender build, passably handsome, and certainly of a pleasing appearance to the young ladies of all classes who passed him, and whose eyes he watched. In front of a coffee house, at a table in the open, he drank Mocha, smoked his cigarettes, and turned the pages of a few illustrated journals, surveying the passers-by, but without actually noticing them. Then, at first gradually, in spite of himself, but of necessity, he awoke to a clear consciousness of actuality. It was five o'clock. Steadily, even if all too slowly, the hours of the afternoon were passing; now undoubtedly the wisest thing to do was to go home and take a good rest, as far as such a thing might be possible. He took the horse-car, descended before his barracks, and, without encountering any unwelcome acquaintance, reached his quarters on the far side of the court. Joseph was in the ante-room, occupied with the Lieutenant's wardrobe, and reported that nothing had occurred, save that Herr von Bogner had been there, shortly before noon, and had left his visiting card. "What do I want with his card?" Willi observed crossly. The card was lying on the table; Bogner had written upon it his private address: Number 20, Piaristengasse. Not far away! Willi reflected. But what does it matter to me, whether he lives near or far, the imbecile! Willi was on the point of tearing up the card, when he changed his mind and tossed it carelessly on the dresser. He turned to his servant: In the evening, between seven and eight, some one would inquire for him; a gentleman, perhaps a gentleman with a lady, perhaps a lady, unaccompanied. "Do you understand?"

"Certainly, Lieutenant."

Willi closed the door, stretched himself

upon the divan—which was a little too short, so that his feet hung over the arm—and sank into slumber as though into an abyss.

XIII

It was already growing dark when the indistinct murmur of a voice aroused him. He opened his eyes and perceived, standing before him, a young lady in a blue and white polka-dot dress. His eyes heavy with sleep, he rose, and as he did so, he saw that his orderly was standing behind the young lady, looking guilty and frightened.

"I must apologize, Lieutenant," he heard Leopoldine's voice say, "for not allowing myself to be announced, but I wished rather to wait until you awakened of your own accord!"

How long has she been here already, Willi wondered, and what am I to assume from her voice? And how different she looks than she did this afternoon! She has surely brought the money! He dismissed

Daybreak

the orderly, who disappeared at once. Then, turning to Leopoldine, he said: "Welcome, Madam! Make yourself comfortable. I am very happy to see you! Please, Madam—" And he invited her to be seated.

She glanced round the room with bright, almost happy eyes, and seemed to like the place. In her hand, she was holding a white and blue striped parasol, which perfectly suited her blue and white polka-dot foulard dress. She wore a straw hat, not of the fashionable wide-brimmed style, but of a Florentine type, with long, drooping, artificial cherries.

"Your place is quite attractive, Lieutenant," she said, and the cherries swung against her ear. "I never imagined that a room in barracks could be so comfortable and neat!"

"They are not all the same," Willi remarked, with some satisfaction.

"In general, I suppose it depends on the occupant!" she added, with a smile.

Willi, embarrassed and happy, set the

books on the table in order, closed the door of a small cabinet, and offered Leopoldine cigarettes from the box which he had purchased at the hotel. She declined, and sat down in the corner of the divan. She looks marvelous! Willi exclaimed to himself. Actually like a lady from a good, respectable family! She reminds one as little of the business woman of this morning as she does of the wild blonde of former times. But where is she carrying the eleven thousand gulden? As if she had surmised his thought, she looked at him smilingly, with an arch expression, and asked an apparently irrelevant question:

"How do you ordinarily live, Lieutenant?"

Then, as Willi hesitated over the proper answer to her entirely too general question, she began to inquire in detail, whether his service was easy or difficult, whether he was soon to be advanced, what were his relations with his superiors, and if he often made excursions into the surrounding country, as, for example, that of the preceding Sunday. Willi replied that his service was sometimes this way and sometimes that way; that his superiors were in general quite pleasant, especially Lieutenant-Colonel Wositzky, who was really quite nice to him; that he could hardly expect a promotion before three years; that he had, of course, very little time for excursions, as Madam could imagine, except on Sundays—and at that, he sighed. Thereupon, Leopoldine, glancing up at him with an infinite cordiality—for he was still standing on the far side of the table—remarked that she hoped that he knew better ways of spending his evenings than in gambling. And how easily she might have added: And while I am on that subject, Lieutenant, let me not forget that I have here the little matter which we spoke about this morning!—But no, not a word, not a motion, to that purpose! She still looked at him smilingly, approvingly, and there was nothing for him to do but to carry on the conversation as well as he could. So he told her of the hospitable Kessner family and of the beautiful villa in which they lived, of the stupid actor, Elrief, of the painted Fräulein Rihoschek, and of the night ride to Vienna in a fiacre.

"I hope you were in good company?" she hazarded.

Oh, not at all; he had gone home with one of his partners! Then she asked, in a teasing voice, whether Fräulein Kessner was blond or dark. He really could not say with certainty, he replied. And his voice intentionally revealed that, in his life, no affairs of the heart held any great significance.

"On the whole, Madam, I think you must imagine my life to be quite different than it actually is!"

Sympathetically, her lips half opened, she looked up to him.

"If one were not so utterly alone," he added, "such fatal ocurrences could not come about!"

She glanced up again with innocent, questioning eyes, as though she did not quite understand him. Then she nodded gravely. But even now she did not make use of the opportunity; and, instead of speaking of the money, which of course she had brought with her—or still more simply, putting the bills on the table without unnecessary words—she remarked: "To stand alone, and to be alone, are two different things!"

"That is too true!" he exclaimed.

And since she nodded understandingly, and since he grew more anxious each time the conversation lagged, he determined to ask her how she had got on all this time, and whether she had had many pleasant experiences. He avoided mentioning the old man whom she had married, and who was his uncle, just as he left out of his conversation any reference to Hornig's and above all, to a certain hotel room, with a dilapidated lattice and a worn pillow with a ruddy shimmer. It was a conversation between a not particularly adroit Lieutenant and a pretty young woman of the middle-class, both of whom knew various things about the other—quite deceptive things—but both of whom had his own reasons for preferring not to touch those subjects, even if the reasons were only to avoid endangering a mood which was not without its charm, and even its promise. Leopoldine had taken off her Florentine hat and laid it upon the table. She still wore the close coiffure of the morning, but she had allowed a few locks of hair to escape and fall in curls upon her temples; and, very remotely, they recalled a former touseled head.

The darkness mounted. Willi was considering whether he ought to light the lamp, which stood in the niche of the white tile stove, when at this moment, he noticed that Leopoldine had taken up her hat again. At first, this did not convey any particular meaning to him, for she had meanwhile begun to tell of an excursion which she had made, the year before, through Mödling, Lilienfeld and Heiligenkreuz, to Baden; but suddenly she put on her Florentine hat, pinned it, and, with a reserved smile, remarked that it was time for her to go. Willi also smiled; but it was an uncertain, almost frightened smile which trembled on his lips. Was she making sport of him? Or did it merely please her to arouse his anxiety, his fear, in order to make him happy at the last moment with the information that she had brought the money with her? Or perhaps she had come with the purpose of excusing herself, of saying that it had not been possible for her to secure the desired sum in cash? And she was simply not able to find the proper words to tell him? In any case, it was unmistakable that she was in earnest about leaving; and in his helplessness, nothing remained to him but to maintain the attitude of a gallant young man who had received a pleasant visit from a young and beautiful woman, and who now found it utterly impossible to let her go at the most interesting moment of their conversation.

"Why do you wish to leave so soon?" he asked, in the voice of a disappointed lover. Then, more urgently: "You don't really wish to leave now, Leopoldine?"

"It is late," she replied. And she added, lightly: "And you doubtless have some better occupation on such a beautiful summer evening!"

He breathed deeply, for she had suddenly begun to speak to him again in the familiar form, and it became difficult for him to keep from betraying his newly mounting hopes. No, he had planned nothing at all, he said; and he had rarely been able to speak with such certainty and with such a clear conscience. She pleaded the formalities, keeping on her hat, and, crossing to the open window, she gazed down with sudden interest into the courtyard below. There was not much to see: there, on the far side, in front of the canteen, soldiers were sitting round a long table; an officer's servant, with a package under his arm, was hurrying across the court; another was pushing a wheelbarrow with a cask of beer toward the canteen; two officers, engrossed in conversation, were walking toward the gate. Willi was standing at Leopoldine's side, somewhat in back of her. Her blue and white polka-dot foulard dress swished lightly; her left arm hung down limply, and at first her hand remained unmoving as his hand touched it, but gradually her fingers slipped between his. From the barracks across the way, through the open window, a trumpet was sounding a melancholy scale. Silence.

"It is rather sad here!" Leopoldine observed at last.

"Do you think so?"

And, as she nodded, he said: "But there is no need for it to be sad!"

Slowly, she turned her head toward him. He had expected to see a smile on her lips, but all that he saw was a delicate, almost unhappy tremor at her lips. Then, abruptly, she turned. "But now it is really high time that I should go!" she exclaimed. "Mary will be waiting for me at table."

"Have you never let Mary wait?" And, since she looked at him smilingly at this last remark, he became bolder and asked her if she would not give him the pleasure of dining this evening in her company. He would send his orderly over to Riedhof's, and she would certainly be home before ten o'clock. Her remonstrances seemed so little in earnest that, without further ado, Willi ran to the ante-room and quickly gave his orderly the necessary instructions. Then he returned at once to Leopoldine.

Although she was still standing at the window, she had just given her Florentine hat a lively swing, so that it flew over the table and dropped upon the bed; and from this moment on, she seemed to be another person. She stroked Willi's smooth head and laughed. He seized her round the waist and drew her down upon the divan. But when he wished to kiss her, she turned away so abruptly that he did not venture any further attempts, but instead asked her how she usually passed her evenings. She looked at him seriously.

"I have so much to do the whole day long," she said, "that I am only too glad to be able to rest at night. I see no one!"

Willi confessed that he could not form any but the vaguest of notions of what her business was really like, and that it puzzled him how she could have entered upon such a career at all. She evaded his questions. He really could not understand such matters. But Willi would not be so easily satisfied; she must at least tell him something of her life—not everything, of course, for that he could not expect, but he would so much like to know, just in general, what had happened since that day when—he had seen her for the last time. Other questions rose to his lips, and his uncle's name as well; but some impulse restrained him, and he did not give them utterance. Without preliminaries, too hastily, he asked her if she were happy.

She looked down. "I think so," she answered softly. "In the first place, I am a free individual; that is what I always wanted to be, more than anything else. I am independent, like—a man!"

"Fortunately, that is the only thing about you which suggests a man," Willi said. He moved closer to her and began to caress her. She allowed him to continue, as if her mind were far away. When the outside door opened, she drew away from him quickly and, rising, took the lamp out of its niche and lit it. Joseph entered with the meal. Leopoldine glanced at what he had brought, and nodded with satisfaction. "The Lieutenant has apparently had experience!" she remarked, smiling. Then she and Joseph together set the table, and, as she would not permit Willi to help, he remained sitting on the divan, "like a pasha," as he remarked, smoking a cigarette. When everything was ready and the hors d'œuvres were served, Joseph was dismissed for the night. Before he left, Leopoldine handed him such a liberal tip that he was utterly taken aback with surprise, and saluted her as if she were a general.

"Your health!" said Willi, and their glasses touched. When they had both drunk, she put aside her glass and pressed her lips passionately against Willi's mouth. And as he became more impetuous, she pushed him away, laughing. "First, let us eat!" she cried, and changed the dishes.

She ate as healthy creatures are accustomed to eat when, having finished their day's work, they indulge themselves in the freedom of accomplished tasks. She ate, with strong, white teeth, but still very delicately and correctly, in the manner of ladies who have now and then eaten in aristocratic restaurants with gentlemen of standing. The bottle of wine was soon emptied, and it was a good thing that the Lieutenant then recollected that he still had half a bottle of French cognac, left over from

God knows what event. After the second glass, Leopoldine appeared to become drowsy. She leaned back in a corner of the divan, and, as Willi bent over her, kissing her eyes, her lips, her neck, she whispered his name, surrendering as if in a dream.

XIV

Day was breaking when Willi awoke, and a cool morning wind was blowing in through the window. But Leopoldine was standing in the middle of the room, completely dressed, her Florentine hat on her head, her parasol in her hand. Willi's first thought was: Good God, how soundly I must have slept! and his second: Where is the money? There she stood, with her hat and parasol, evidently prepared to leave the room within the next minute. She nodded her head in a morning greeting. He stretched out his arms toward her, as if in longing. She approached, sat down on the edge of the bed, and gazed at him with a friendly but severe countenance. He wanted to embrace her, to draw her to him, but she pointed to her hat and to the parasol which she held in her hand as if it were a weapon, and shook her head. "No more nonsense!" she said, and attempted to arise. But he restrained her.

"You don't intend to go?" he asked, and his voice was almost tearful.

"Certainly!" she replied, and passed her hand over his hair in a sisterly caress. "I would like to get a few hours of rest. I have an important conference at nine o'clock."

It suddenly occurred to Willi that this might be a conference—what a sound that word had!—to discuss his affair; the consultation with the lawyer, which she probably had not had the time to take care of yesterday. In his impatience, he asked her at once.

"A conference with your lawyer?"

"No," she replied with ease, "I am awaiting a business friend from Prague."

She bent over him, pushed his little mustach away from his lips, and gave him a hasty kiss. "Good-bye!" she whispered, and arose. In the next moment she might be outside the door! Willi's heart stood still. She wanted to go? She wanted to go, just like that! But a new hope awoke within him. Perhaps she had discreetly put the money somewhere! Timidly, his eyes wandered round the room—from the table to the niche in the stove. Perhaps she had hidden it under the pillow while he was sleeping! Instinctively, his hand sought the place. Nothing! Or perhaps she had put it in his wallet, which was lying near his watch! If he could only look! And all the while, he could feel, he knew, he could see, how she was following his movements, with derision, with malice. Their eyes met, for the merest fraction of a second. He turned his eyes away, as if he had been detected in some unworthy act. Her hand was already on the door-knob. He wanted to call out her name, but his voice would not come, as in a nightmare one cannot speak. He had an impulse to leap out of bed, to throw himself at her, to hold her back; yes, he was ready to run after her on the steps, in his night-shirt—

exactly—he could see the picture in his mind—as he had once seen a prostitute run after a man in a provincial bordello, many years ago, because he had not paid her loveprice . . . But Leopoldine, as if she had heard her name, which he had not spoken aloud, kept one hand on the knob and, with the other, felt in the pocket of her dress.

"I had almost forgotten!" she said casually, and drawing near again, she put a bill on the table. "There!" she said—and was already back at the door.

With a single, spasmodic movement, Willi was sitting on the edge of the bed, staring at the bill. It was only a single bill, a thousand gulden bill—there were no higher denominations; it could not be more than a thousand!

"Leopoldine!" he cried, in a strange, unnatural voice. But when she turned round at his call, her hand still on the knob, and looked at him with a surprised and frigid glance, he was covered with deep, anguished shame, such as never before in his

Daybreak

life he had experienced. But now it was too late; he had to go on, no matter where it led him, no matter how black the ignominy. And his lips cried uncontrollably:

"But that is too little, Leopoldine! I did not ask for a thousand! Perhaps you misunderstood me yesterday. I asked for eleven thousand!" And, involuntarily, beneath the gaze of her cold eyes, he pulled the covers over his naked legs.

She stared at him as though she had not quite understood him; then she nodded her head several times, as if it were all clear to her now. "Oh, yes," she said, "you thought . . ."—and she inclined her head contemptuously toward the bill—"That has nothing to do with your request. The thousand gulden are not a loan; they belong to you—for last night!" And between her half open lips, her moist tongue played with her sparkling teeth.

The cover slipped from Willi's legs. He stood erect. The blood mounted to his head and burned in his eyes. She looked at him calmly, curiously. And, as he was unable to utter a word, she asked: "But that is not too little? What did you expect? A thousand gulden! You gave me only ten! Do you still remember?" He advanced a few steps toward her. Leopoldine remained calmly standing at the door. With a sudden movement, he seized the bill, crumpling it in his trembling fingers, as if he were about to throw it at her feet. Then she released the knob, stepped up to him, and looked straight into his eyes.

"That was not to be taken as a reproach," she said. "I had no right to expect more at that time. Ten gulden—was plenty. In fact, too much!" Her eyes held his. "To speak accurately, it was precisely ten gulden too much!"

He stared at her, then looked away, beginning to understand.

"I could not know that!" he said, in a low voice.

"You might have seen it!" she answered, "It was not so difficult to see!"

He looked at her again; and now he was aware of a strange radiance in the depths of her eyes—the same childish and beautiful radiance that he remembered having seen in her eyes on that night long past, so many years ago. And now all his memories were revivified—and he recalled not only the pleasure which she had given him, as others before had given him pleasure, and many others since, and the caressing words she had spoken, just as others had spoken them, but also the wonderful surrender, such as he had never experienced since, with which she had put her slender, childish arms about him and had said, in accents that now sounded again across the years: "Don't leave me alone! I love you!"— words, words such as he had never heard from any other. He had forgotten all this. Now he remembered it again. And now— he knew! that what she had done today was just what he had done then. Undisturbed, thoughtlessly, while she still slumbered in sweet lassitude, he had arisen from her side, and reflected hastily if a smaller bill would not do, and then nobly put down a ten gulden bill on her table. Then, feeling the anxious look of the slowly awakening girl, still drunk with sleep, he had run quickly away to snatch a few hours of rest in the barracks. And in the morning, even before he had gone to his duties, he had forgotten the little flower girl from Hornig's.

Meanwhile, however, while this dim light became so surprisingly alive, the childish, beautiful radiance had gradually faded from Leopoldine's eyes. Now she stared at him with cold, grey, distant eyes; and, as the picture of that night vanished from his mind, anger, aversion, and exasperation arose in its place. What did she think she was doing? How could she presume so far, as if she really believed that he had actually offered himself to her for money? How dared she treat him like a gigolo, who sold his favours? And she had the effrontery to add to such an unheard-of insult the most insolent disdain, by bargaining for a lower price than the one which had been set—like a lover who has been displeased at his mistress's incapacity! Perhaps she doubted that he would have thrown the entire eleven thousand back at her, if she had dared to offer it to him as the wage of love!

But even as the foul word, which was due her, was finding its way to his lips; as he lifted his fist, as if to crush beneath it the miserable creature before him, the word failed him, his hand sank slowly to his side. For he suddenly became aware—perhaps he had suspected it all the while?—that he had been prepared to sell himself. And not alone to her, but to any other, to any one at all, who might have offered him the sum which could save him; and thus, in the cruel and treacherous wrong which had been added to his store of misery by an evil woman, he began to see, in the depths of his soul, despite himself, a hidden, inescapable justice, which had ensnarled him, not only in this sorry adventure, but in the very essence of his life.

He looked up; he looked round the room; he felt as if he were awakening from a confused dream. Leopoldine had gone. He had not yet opened his mouth—and already she was gone. He could not understand how she had contrived to leave the room so suddenly—without his having seen. He felt the crumpled bill in his still taut fingers. Dashing to the window, he threw it wide open, as if he wished to fling the thousand gulden after her. There she was! He would have called after her, but she was already far away. She was walking along the wall, her step lilting and joyous, with her parasol in her hand and her Florentine hat—walking along, as if she had come from some night of love, as no doubt she had come from hundreds of others. She was at the gate. The guard saluted her, as if she were a person of rank, and then she disappeared.

Willi shut the window and stepped back

Daybreak

into the room. He noticed the disturbed bed, the remnants of the meal on the table, the empty glasses and bottles. Involuntarily, his hand opened, and the bill fell. He caught a glimpse of himself in the mirror above the dresser—his tangled hair, the dark rings under his eyes—and he shuddered. It annoyed him unspeakably that he was still in his night-shirt. He took down his overcoat from the hook, pulled it on, buttoned it, and turned up the collar. He strode aimlessly up and down the room several times. Suddenly he stood, as if rooted, before the dresser. In the middle drawer, between the handkerchiefs, he knew his revolver lay. Well, he had got that far, at least! As far as the other, who had perhaps already gone beyond it. Or was Bogner still waiting for a miracle? At any rate, he, Willi, had done his share, and even more. And at this moment, it veritably seemed to him that he had sat down at the card table for Bogner's sake alone, and that he had tempted fate so very long for Bogner's sake alone, until he had himself become a victim.

The bill still lay on a dish among the half consumed pastry, just as it had dropped from his hand a moment before, and it did not even look particularly crumpled. It had begun to unfold itself; it would not be long before it would be smooth, as smooth as any other cleaner paper, and no one would be able to tell that it was nothing better than the wages of sin—shame-money! Well, whatever the circumstances, it belonged to him—to his estate, so to speak. He smiled bitterly. He might bequeath it to whomever he wished—and he should leave it to the one who had the best right to it. Bogner, more than any other! He burst into laughter. Excellent! That matter would be taken care of, in any case! It was to be hoped that Bogner had not killed himself too early. The miracle had actually happened—for him! All that he had had to do was to wait for it.

But where was Joseph? He knew that there was an expedition scheduled for to-day. Willi should have been ready at three o'clock to join it. It was now half-past four. The regiment had long since gone. But he had not heard it, his sleep had been so deep. He opened the door to the ante-room. His orderly was sitting there on a stool, near the little iron stove. Joseph stood at attention.

"I wish to report, Sir, that I have reported the Lieutenant ill."

"Ill? Who told you to do that? . . . Oh, yes—of course!"—Leopoldine!—She might just as well have given the order to report him dead; it would have been simpler. "Very well! Get me a cup of coffee," he said, and closed the door.

Where could that visiting card be? He searched through all the drawers, on the floor, in all the corners, as though his own life depended on it. In vain! He could not find it. It was not to be! Bogner was simply condemned to ill-luck; their fates were inextricably bound. Suddenly, he saw a white something glistening in the niche. There was the card, with the address on it: Number 20, Piaristengasse—quite nearby! And what if it had been further! So this Bogner had luck, after all! Suppose he had been unable to find the card!

He took the bill, examined it without really seeing it, folded it, inserted it into a sheet of paper, reflected for a moment whether he ought not to write a few explanatory words, then shrugged his shoulders. "To what end?" he murmured. He wrote the address on the envelope: "Herr Oberleutnant Otto von Bogner." Oberleutnant! To be sure! He gave the fellow back his old commission, upon his own authority. One always remained an officer, no matter what one did—or, at any rate, one became an officer again, when one had paid one's debts!

He called his orderly and gave him the letter to deliver. "And quickly!"

"Any answer, Lieutenant?"

"No. See to it that you give it to him

Daybreak

personally, and—no answer! And whatever happens, don't wake me up when you return. . . . Let me sleep until I wake up by myself."

"Very good, Sir!"

Joseph clicked his heels, turned smartly about, and hastened off. On the steps, he could hear the sound of the key being turned in the door.

XV

Three hours later, there was a ring at the hall door. Joseph, who had returned long since and had fallen asleep, awoke with a start and opened. There stood Bogner—the gentleman to whom, three hours earlier, he had delivered the letter with which his master had dispatched him.

"Is the Lieutenant at home?"

"I am sorry, but the Lieutenant is still sleeping."

Bogner looked at his watch. Immediately after the accountants had examined his books, he had taken an hour off, in his anxiety to render thanks to his saviour. He paced up and down the small ante-room. "Has he no duties today?"

"The Lieutenant is ill."

The Army Doctor, Tugut, suddenly appeared in the door, which was still open. "Does Lieutenant Kasda live here?" he demanded.

"Yes, Sir."

"May I speak with him?"

"I beg to report, Sir, that the Lieutenant is sleeping now. He is ill."

"Please announce me. Army Doctor Tugut!"

"I beg to report, Sir, that the Lieutenant gave orders that he was not to be disturbed!"

"It is an urgent matter. Go and awaken the Lieutenant. I will be responsible."

As Joseph, with some hesitation, knocked at the door, Tugut looked suspiciously at the civilian who was standing there. Bogner presented himself. The Army Doctor had heard the name before, and knew of the painful scandal connected with it. But of this he gave no sign, and presented himself in return. They did not shake hands.

There was no response from Lieutenant Kasda. Joseph knocked more loudly, put his ear to the door, shrugged his shoulders, and said, as if to quiet his own fears: "The Lieutenant is always a sound sleeper!"

Bogner and Tugut glanced at one another, and one of the barriers between them was broken. Then the Army Doctor stepped up to the door and called out Kasda's name. There was no answer. "Strange!" Tugut muttered, his brow wrinkling, and he twisted the knob in vain.

Joseph stood with pale face and eyes wide open.

"Go fetch the regimental locksmith, quickly!" Tugut commanded.

"Yes, Sir!"

Bogner and Tugut were alone.

"Incomprehensible!" Bogner observed.

"You know about it, Herr von Bogner?" Tugut demanded.

"You mean, do I know of his gambling losses?" And, as Tugut nodded: "Yes, of course!"

"I wanted to learn how the affair stood," Tugut began hesitatingly; "whether he had succeeded in obtaining the money. Perhaps you know, Herr von Bogner?"

"I know nothing," Bogner replied.

Tugut went to the door again, shook it, and called out Kasda's name. No answer.

Bogner, who had been watching through the window, announced: "Here comes Joseph with the locksmith!"

"You were his comrade?" Tugut asked.

Bogner answered, out of the corner of his mouth: "I am the one you are thinking of!"

Tugut paid no attention to the remark. "It sometimes happens that, after great excitement . . ." He began again—"I rather suspect that he had no sleep this past night, either."

"Yesterday at noon," Bogner observed, with assurance, "he certainly did not have the money, as yet——"

Tugut looked at Bogner in a way that the latter interpreted as questioning whether perhaps he, Bogner, had not brought the money. So Bogner said, as if in answer to this unspoken question: "Nor, unfortunately, did I succeed in getting the money!"

Joseph appeared, accompanied by the locksmith, a young man in the uniform of the regiment, stocky and red-cheeked, carrying the necessary implements. Tugut knocked once more at the door, violently—a last attempt. They all stood by, holding their breath. There was no sound.

"Very well, then." Tugut turned to the locksmith with a gesture of command, and the latter set to work immediately. His task did not take long. In a few seconds, the door was opened. Lieutenant Willi Kasda, in his overcoat, with his collar raised, was reclining in the corner of the black leather divan, his eyes half closed, his head upon his breast, his right arm relaxed and hanging over the side of the couch, the revolver lying on the floor. From his temple, a narrow stream of dark red blood had trickled over his cheek, disappearing between his neck and the collar of his coat. Prepared as they all were, they were nevertheless deeply moved by the spectacle. The Army Doctor drew near, lifted the drooping arm, let it go, and it dropped once more over the side. Then Tugut unbuttoned Kasda's coat. The crumpled shirt beneath was open wide. Mechanically, Bogner stooped to pick up the revolver. "Halt!" Tugut exclaimed, his ear on the naked breast of the dead man. "Everything must remain as it is!" Joseph and the locksmith still stood motionless at the open door. The locksmith shrugged his shoulders and looked at Joseph with a half deprecatory, half frightened glance, as if he felt himself responsible for the sight which had appeared behind the door which he had violated.

Steps were heard below—at first slow, then increasingly rapid, until they ceased. Bogner turned at once. An old man appeared near the leaning door, dressed in a light and somewhat worn summer suit, with something of the manner of a soured actor about him. Hesitatingly, he looked about.

"Herr Wilram!" Bogner exclaimed. "His uncle!" he whispered to the Army Doctor, who had straightened up from his examination of the body.

But Robert Wilram did not at once grasp what had happened. He saw his nephew lying in the corner of the divan, with his limp arm hanging down, and he made a step forward, as if to go to him. He no doubt suspected that something terrible had taken place, but he refused to credit it. The Army Doctor held him back.

"A most lamentable thing has happened! But there is nothing more that can be done." And as the other stared at him, unable to understand, he continued: "My name is Tugut. I am an Army Doctor. Death must have occurred several hours ago."

Robert Wilram—his behaviour struck everybody as being extremely peculiar—suddenly pulled an envelope out of his pocket and waved it in the air. "But I have got it here, Willi!" he cried. "Here is the money, Willi! Here is the money, Willi!" he continued, as if he actually imagined that he could thus bring back the life which had departed. "She gave it to me this morning! The whole eleven thousand! Here they are!" And he turned round to the others, as though calling them to witness this portentous fact. "This is the entire amount, Gentlemen—eleven thousand gulden!"— as though, now that they knew that he had brought the money, they would at least make some attempt to revive the dead man.

"It is too late, unfortunately!" the Army Doctor said gently. He turned to Bogner. "I am going to make my report." Then he commanded: "The body is to remain as it is!" And, turning to the orderly, he added severely: "You will be responsible! See to it that everything remains as it is!" And before he left, he turned round once more and shook hands with Bogner.

Bogner wondered: Where did he get that

thousand for me? He noticed the table, the glasses, the dishes, and the empty bottles. Two glasses . . . Did he have a woman with him, then, his last night?

Joseph crossed to the divan, near the body of his dead master. He stood stiffly erect, like a guard. Nevertheless, he did not forbid Robert Wilram, when the latter suddenly went up to the body, with the envelope still in his clasped hand, and pleaded: "Willi!" He shook his head in despair. Then he sank to his knees before his dead nephew; and so near was he to the naked breast that he detected a strangely familiar perfume wafted in his direction from the crumpled shirt. He inhaled it deeply, and looked up into the dead man's face, as though he were tempted to ask him a question.

From the court below came the rythmical beat of the returning regiment, marching in order. Bogner was anxious to make his departure before some of his former com-

Daybreak

rades entered the room, as they were likely to do. In any case, his presence was superfluous. He cast a farewell glance at the body, which was reclining stiffly in the corner of the divan; and, followed by the locksmith, he hastened down the steps. He waited before the gate until the regiment had passed; then, pressing close to the wall, he crept away.

Robert Wilram still remained on his knees before his dead nephew. He looked round the room and, for the first time, noticed the table and observed the remains of the meal—the plates, the bottles, the glasses. In one of them there was still a moist, golden-yellow shimmer. He asked the servant: "Did the Lieutenant entertain last night?"

There were steps outside. Confused voices. Robert Wilram rose.

"Yes, Sir," Joseph replied, still standing erect, like a guard. "Until late at night . . . a gentleman, an old comrade. . . ."

And the unreasonable thought which had suddenly come to the old man, vanished.

The voices and the steps came nearer.

Joseph stood more stiffly erect than ever. The committee entered the room.